LETTERS

— FROM —

BRAZIL
II

Research, Romance,
and Dark Days Ahead

MARK J. CURRAN

Order this book online at www.trafford.com
or email orders@trafford.com

Most Trafford titles are also available at major online book retailers.

The names of all principal characters in this narrative are fictitious. Writers and composers, Ariano Suassuna and Chico Buarque de Hollanda among them are real personages in Brazil. So are military figures like Colonel Manuel Cavalcanti Proença, General Castelo Branco, General Costa e Silva, General Garrastazu Médici, and Finance Minister Delfim Neto and other Brazilian officials. However, none of the episodes involving Brazilian acquaintances, writers, musicians, politicians, military leaders or government employees with Mike Gaherty in this narrative are real. They are all the result of the author's imagination.

Print information available on the last page.

ISBN: 978-1-4907-9359-7 (sc)
ISBN: 978-1-4907-9360-3 (e)

Trafford rev. 02/05/2019

www.trafford.com

North America & international
toll-free: 1 888 232 4444 (USA & Canada)
fax: 812 355 4082

PART I

1968 -1969

EPIGRAPH

"A política é um prato perigoso hoje em dia" (José Costa Leite, a Poet from the "Literatura de Cordel")

"Politics Is A Dangerous Plate These Days" ["Plate of the Day"]

THE POLITICAL
REALITY IN BRAZIL

The Brazilian Military Revolution had begun in April 1964, and its first military president, General Castelo Branco, had instituted the military's form of governance with Institutional Act I. It established the taking away of political rights for ten years, including of those holding office as "enemies of the regime," and established the right of the Military to govern by decree. Even Brazil's national hero, Juscelino Kubitschek, founder of Brasília and the national economic growth, was put on the list of the "cassados" [those with rights taken away]." The regime had as its goals to combat Communism, subversive action against the Fatherland in the form of peasant revolts in the Northeast and student protests, and to return to and maintain Brazil's motto of "Order and Progress" while maintaining the values of God and family.

AI -2 (Institutional Act n. 2) came in October 1965. All political parties were declared to be illegal. Instead the Military established two new political parties: ARENA of the government ("Aliança Renovadora Nacional") and an opposition party the MDB ("Movimento Democrático Brasileiro") the second really a "token" party only given lip service when the Military deemed necessary. And finally, it was announced that the next presidential election would be "indirect," that is, a procedure carried out within the military hierarchy. AI-2 in effect converted the military president into a dictator.

It was at this time Brazil aligned itself with the United States (Brazilian presidents as early as Jânio Quadros had awarded Brazil's highest honor to dictator Fidel Castro in 1960, and then João Goulart led a leftist leaning regime of 1961 to 1964), broke relations with Cuba, and sent troops to the Dominican Republic in support of the U.S. invasion. The SNI [National Information Service] became the "data bank" for the nation. And a national program of economic austerity was ushered in in late 1965. (This was all before I, Mike Gaherty, did initial travel and research in Brazil.)

The first act of terrorism had been July 25th, 1966 when a terrorist bomb went off in Guararapes Airport in Recife, narrowly missing killing the military presidential "candidate" General Costa e Silva, already chosen to replace General Castelo Branco. (I, Mike Gaherty, was in Recife when this happened and told of the event as reported in a "Cordel" story-poem.) In November 1966 the government fired six congressmen when the congress refused to accept new military regulations, and shortly thereafter President Castelo Branco temporarily closed the congress. Opposition to the government, what there was of it, was now called the "Frente Ampla" ["Wide Front"].

The Costa e Silva government (after I had left Brazil and "Letters from Brazil" was published in New York in 1967) began suppressing the progressive liberals of the Catholic Church. The clerics of the "Liberation Theology" became targets; a Jesuit priest was murdered in Recife and Brazil's leading progressive Bishop Dom Hêlder Câmara was attacked in the same city, his home hit by machine gun bullets in a drive by shooting (intended as a warning).

And then they went after the members of the UNE [National Student Union] throughout 1968. After a student member was killed in a demonstration in Rio de Janeiro, the government prohibited all further demonstrations. The Brazilians reacted and the famous "Demonstration of the 100,000" ["Passeata dos Cem Mil"] took place in June 1968. Negotiations failed, and the federal police invaded the campus of the University of Brasília in August of 1968 and shut it down. Later that month the city of São Paulo dissolved the 30th Congress of the UNE and closed the UNE protest that followed. Students were arrested, and congress protested. The culmination of it all was AI – 5 on December 13, 1968. The national congress was permanently dissolved with more "cassações" of its members' political rights and complete press censorship became the rule of the times.

One major aspect of AI – 5 was the institution of "censura previa" ["pre-censorship"] in the press and arts in Brazil. This backfired on the Generals as the Brazilians developed an uncanny way of fooling the government ["driblando a censura," a soccer term]. The role of the composers and artists of the immensely popular MPB, Brazilian Popular Music and the reporters of the major newspapers became central to daily life under the repression and part of this story.

Other than that, Brazil was still the land of the beaches, "futebol" and carnival.

This is the reality in 1969 when Mike Gaherty will return to Brazil.

1

MIKE GAHERTY IN LINCOLN

I'm Mike Gaherty, now an Assistant Professor of Spanish and Portuguese at the University of Nebraska in Lincoln, busting my butt (contrary to what most of the public thinks) teaching a full load of language classes five days a week during the day and an extra course on Tuesday and Thursday nights. Since I'm still basically a "rookie," no upper division or graduate literature or civilization courses are open to me. That doesn't change one basic scary reality – academic publication! I'm making my way in academia working toward tenure in its "publish or perish" atmosphere, and the vehicle to get there also involves good teaching and "citizenship in the university," in other words, working on boring department and college committees and not offending the senior professors on the same. In addition, even though I'm teaching Spanish and Portuguese, Introduction to Spanish Literature and Brazilian Literature, I've got to come up with ideas to keep Portuguese enrollment up and that means sponsoring "The Brazil Club."

Even though the university insists on all the above, fine teaching, university service, what really counts is the publication list. This will come with continued research on Brazilian Culture and its Folk-Popular Poetry, "A Literatura de Cordel." I'm hoping that in 1969 I can return to Brazil for such work. Nebraska is on the "make" (relatively) and wants its share of a national reputation as a "great public research university." So, to take up any "spare time" I'm retooling the Ph.D. dissertation into chapters to submit as articles in academic reviews and shaping up the entire thing as a small book to peddle in Brazil.

What the reader does not know is what I wrote in the dissertation and needs to be seen to understand this story. In effect, I must tell what I had learned in 1966-1967 (told in "Letters in Brazil") and some important developments in the folk poetry, many happening before 1966 but discovered when I got down to the dissertation research back at Georgetown in Washington D.C. in 1967 and 1968. It turns out "Cordel" was "preparing the way" for the new research. That mass of story-poems I had collected in the dusty markets of the backlands of the Northeast and the northeastern fair in Rio would provide the "preamble" to a possible return to Brazil.

As early as the very beginning of the military rule, a regime that would evolve in just a few short years to totally divide the nation, the "Cordel" reported on, gave opinions from its humble folk-popular poets and really provided a "folk-popular" journalism and historic account of major events after April 1, 1964 when the Military seized power from the leftist leaning João "Jango" Goulart and with its hard-liner generals "saved" Brazil from the Red Peril, Fidel Castro, Miguel Arraes, the leftist governor of Pernambuco State, and Francisco Julião, the leftist land-reform politician in the poverty-stricken Northeast.

"Jango and the Reforms" was a "Cordel" story-poem telling of the proposed huge land reform proposal by the Goulart administration, one of the lynchpins of the Left in the early 1960s. The reforms were a lethal blow to the old oligarchic landholders who still controlled rural Brazil and had big time support from the hard-liners in the military. The Right saw them as an imitation of Fidel Castro's massive land reform in Cuba. They were in large part the straw that broke the camel's back and brought the coup of April 1, 1964. Incidentally, João Cabral de Melo Neto's "Christmas Play" ["Auto de Natal"] "Morte e Vida Severina" ["A Severe Life and Death"] would have a somber but beautiful passage with the same theme – land reform.

Stories like "The Democratic Victory and the Rosary" written and printed shortly after the Revolution, or at least coup originally, linked the revolution, soon to be called "The Redeemer" ["A Redentora"] to of course saving democracy as an institution and the Catholic faith and tradition as the bulwark in the 1960s against atheistic Communism. A like title, also in 1964, "The Victory of Democracy and the Defeat of Communism" shared similar feelings. One must understand that the poets of "Cordel" mirrored the vastly conservative stance of most people in Brazil. "You write to please your buyers" was the mantra to survive in the rough and tumble "cordel" market.

Yet in 1965 "cordel" got personal with the title "The Government of Marechal Castelo Branco - the Defeat of the Corrupt," Castelo Branco, Brazil's first military president, soon to become dictator. Both AI – 1 and AI -2 were presented to Brazilians by decree during that time. It was AI- 2, recall from our introduction, in October when all past political parties were determined to be illegal, and the generals instituted ARENA [National Renovating Alliance) and MNDB, [National Movement of

Brazilian Democracy] the respective government and token opposition parties. The president had become a dictator. The story-poem reported, as already seen in our preface, that Brazil, formerly with diplomatic relations with Castro's Cuba, cut those relations and linked itself to the USA, even sending Brazilian troops to the Dominican Republic to fight alongside U.S. troops to restore democracy in that poor Caribbean Island Nation.

And "Cordel" would report on the SNI (National Information Service) which was begun in Brazil and became the main instrument of repression, via its national data bank. The generals brought austerity to the economy with the monetary unit the "cruzeiro novo" ["new 'cruzeiro'"] and economist Roberto Campos's plan: "a big cake for Brazil" with slices even for the poor (it did not happen).

It wasn't just politics or economics. A series of events and persons converged, aspects from a really memorable phase in all cordelian history in the decade of the 1960s : the arrival of "rock n' roll," the advent of the "jovem guarda" of Brazilian musicians like Roberto Carlos and Erasmo Carlos with their "iê-iê-iê" ["yeah, yeah, yeah"] music, the Beatles in Brazil, the "hippie" generation in the United States, and above all, a profound change in customs, represented by the "long-hairs" ["cabeludos"] and by new changes in clothes styles. In this vein an old, traditional topic of popular folkloric literature was renewed: the moral example lamenting modern times and preaching a return to a mythical "Golden Age" when everything was better.

This coincided with "war" against the immorality of atheistic communism. When I, Mike Gaherty, arrived in June 1966 there was a flood of "Cordel" stories, mostly from right-wing conservative Rodolfo Coelho Cavalcante, lamenting the loss of the "good 'ole days" (a perennial theme of folklore in the western world and cordelian theme by the way) and the evils of the changing times. Rodolfo had good reason to hate the Communists. When he refused to write a propaganda story-poem for the election in Maceió, Alagoas, his home state, backing the Communist candidate, thugs hired by the latter caught up with the poet one day, beat him up, tied him up with rope and tossed him into a nearby canal to drown. Somehow or other Rodolfo escaped the bonds and never forgot the incident. His poetry became a campaign against the Left. One such indicative title from 1966 was "The Result of the Long Hairs Today" railing against the changing social mores including dress and hair style brought on by the Beatles and Brazil's own home -grown rockers Roberto Carlos and Erasmo Carlos. "The Scandalous Styles of Today" was in the same vein. Rodolfo once told one of his sons, "If you come home with long hair, you'll get the beating of your life!" The best example summarizing the entire period was Rodolfo's "The Result of All the

Long-Hairs of Today" ["O Resultado dos Cabeludos de Hoje em Dia"] in December of 1966. It is his conclusion after railing against the new morality and change that hit the public between the eyes: "That is why the world is living in such confusion; it is Communism infiltrating and bringing revolution. They are setting off bombs here, killing government officials there, and all with no compassion. Field Marshall Costa e Silvia our future president will know how to deal with this. A country without order cannot have progress; where there is no respect there can be no order. I praise any authority than can bring a change to this."

I wrote of some of this in "Letters from Brazil" including reporting on the terrorist bombing of Guararapes Airport in Recife and the narrow escape with his life from "President-Elect" General Costa e Silva." In December 1966, yet president Castelo Branco closed congress (temporarily) for refusing to accept the firing of six federal deputies. It was about this time the opposition became known as the "Frente Ampla" or "Wide Front."

Yet in December of that year, my first in Brazil, a wonderful book excoriating the feeble and foolish efforts of the military to regulate morality came out: "Festival of Idiocy that Runs Rampant in the Nation" ["Festival da Besteira que Assola o País"] by Stanislaw Ponte Preta, pen name for Sérgio Porto. The Military had condemned kissing and public affection in the small and large towns and cities' plazas by the general public.

In 1967 one minor yet important event took place in Rio de Janeiro. The popular local paper "Tribuna da Imprensa" dared to make one of the strongest attacks on the national government and the incipient dictatorship. Headed by its editor, Hélio Fernandes, the newspaper did a count-down, day by day in successively reduced numbers: 10, 9, 8, … and finally the daily with a huge red number 1 on the front cover: "One more day until President Castelo Branco Leaves Office." On the back cover were all the worst possible photos of the General, called "No – Necked Castelo" ["Castelo Sem Pescoço"]. For his trouble, journalist Fernandes was jailed, his political rights taken away and the newspaper closed. Incidentally, the young teenager Chico Buarque de Hollanda did a song at the time about "no-necked Castelo," but did not yet suffer the wrath of censorship. He flew under the radar.

All the above was on my mind in shaping up the dissertation for possible publication. It's not as though there weren't other things going on at home and across the country. Martin Luther King assassinated! Robert Kennedy assassinated! The riots in Chicago! The Viet Nam morass! All in 1968. I'll admit I had my head in the sand most of the time. It's a poor defense but that "nose to the grindstone" effort at the university and the fight for tenure frankly trumped what was going on around me.

Oh yeah, and loneliness. I dated a "blond bombshell" teaching assistant from the language department at U. of N off and on and one time got lucky when I took her for a drive to the boonies in my old beat up Chrysler 300 (inherited from my DUI brother), got it on a time or two (funny but I remember best her Nebraska "Big Red" bra and panties), but then she jilted me for a better offer – a TWA Airlines Pilot. A bit more exotic than a stuffy language and culture teacher spending most of his time in the library. But it was after that on a trip back to D.C. for the Georgetown graduation ceremony with obligatory "hooding" by my Jesuit Ph.D. advisor that I reconnected with a sweet gal I met at a graduate school party in D.C. in my last year at Georgetown. Things moved pretty fast. She was smart, good looking with an imposing figure, a full-length lynx coat and a new car, doing a whole lot better dollar wise than I was. But we clicked, and I guess a Ph.D. and a job at a good university appealed to her intellectual side. And we were both Catholic. She certainly played her cards right; we were both on track for a future together that year of 1969. There was one, uh, complication. The reader might remember Cristina Maria in Rio. She was the girl I met on Ipanema beach, the one who inspired me to love MPB and Chico Buarque Music, the one who turned me on in the back booth of the "Castelinhno" bar in Ipanema during those hot summer nights in Rio in 1967, and incidentally the daughter of that leftist "cassado" politician that got me in trouble with the DOPS.

2

NYT - INR -WHA

So, I need to get back to Brazil. One minor problem: I have to find research funding and it's not easy. Even though I had the NDEA Fellowship at Georgetown from 1963 to 1966 for the Ph.D. and the prestigious Fulbright-Hays Grant to Brazil for research in 1966-1967 and am now employed at a state university, albeit a good one, it's not Harvard or Yale. Summer or even annual grant proposals for funding from NEH (National Endowment of the Humanities) or The American Philosophical Society in Philadelphia are usually chosen by panels of professors from the Ivy Leagues or western "heavy-weights" like Berkeley or Stanford, so Nebraska is not exactly a household word with those folks. The only recourse in 1969 is a summer research grant, a paltry $2000 from Nebraska, just enough to pay air fare and modest living expenses, and even then, the competition is fierce. Good things happen, and I get that grant for 1969 for a month or two in Brazil.

Fortunately, my "Letters from Brazil" for James Hansen of the International Section of the "New York Times" in 1966-1967 was well received as was the contribution to the State Department's Bureau of International Research – Western Hemisphere Analisis's [INR - WHA] interests. As soon as I got the Nebraska summer grant, I contacted Mr. Hansen with the good news. He wants a continuation of the "Letters" and is joined as well by Iverson of the INR-WHA, all this resulting in me being given diplomatic status by the latter as a "researcher - journalist." There will even be a small retainer to be received at the end of the summer. My role is to report on cultural activity and "Cordel" production that reflect the political, social, religious and cultural reality of the time. I hope to give New Yorkers and the readers of the "Times" across the world a colorful, entertaining, and informative narrative of Brazil as it grows in economic, political and cultural importance on the world stage, moving from an emerging Third World Nation to a major player representing much of Latin America to the world. The nuts and bolts of the reporting will have many facets: my experiences in Brazil, daily life in Brazil in diverse cities and locations, chronicling the story-poems of "Cordel" that reflect the national reality, but just as important, enthusiasm for the MPB [Brazilian Popular Music] and its role in the evolution of Brazil from the beginnings of the dictatorship in 1966-1967.

The Brazilian SNI - "Serviço Nacional de Informação" [National Information Service] and DOPS – "Departamento de Ordem Política e Social" [Department of Social and Political Order] are aware of this new status and approve of it as long as I do not interfere with internal politics in Brazil and simply report happenings as a U.S. employee.

I hope to avoid my penchant for getting into scrapes, tight spots and being at the wrong place at the wrong time, thus complicating my legal cover with the INR-WHA and its tenuous relationship with the regime. And to avoid complications with Brazilian women.

3

VARIG TO BRAZIL

June 1969. This time I flew on the famous Varig Airlines, the route from Miami to Belém do Pará and on to Recife which would be my "base camp" for this year's research. Oh, I forgot; before I go on, I want you to know the plan with Molly.

I told her in a quick visit to D.C. before a departure to Miami, Recife in June and Rio in July that I really didn't know what would happen, but I had to find out if the Brazil flame with Cristina Maria was still burning, and at both ends. Kind of a crappy way to put it, and maybe not too kind, but the truth. So, I left Molly in a teary goodbye at Dulles.

The service on Varig was the well-known of the times: gum drops or Chiclets before taking off, the steaming hot towel to "refresh oneself" before the first meal, slippers to ease the swollen feet during the long flight, beautiful maps of Brazil and Varig's routes throughout the world, the day's newspapers and magazines and then the meal itself: pre-dinner cocktails and appetizers ["tira-gostos"], the first course of salad and salmon, the main course of filet mignon with potatoes and vegetables, and then the pastry for dessert and the excellent and fine aroma of Brazilian demitasse coffee ("cafezinho"). All was accompanied (I like the Brazilian word from novelist Jorge Amado: "regado" – "irrigated") with pre-dinner drinks, wine during the meal and liqueurs later. Wonderful! What a way to toast our imminent arrival in Brazil. And this all was in economy-tourist class. Stewards and stewardesses were spiffy and smart in their Varig Uniforms.

We arrived at the International Airport of Belém do Pará at 2:30 a.m. There was the usual bureaucracy – too many passengers, too few airline employees to handle them all and the resulting slow and inefficient scene at the airline counter. There was one agent to attend to all the passengers traveling on to various cities in Brazil: he was to check passports and visas, see the original international tickets and issue new tickets and boarding passes to the Brazilian destinations, and on top of that make sure the luggage stickers were properly done. The poor fellow was sweating profusely, visibly nervous, checking each airline ticket (you had a cardboard coupon for each destination, international and national; it could amount to a good sized stack), rechecking the same, forgetting what he had already seen, trying to deal with luggage, cleaning and recleaning his glasses and swearing at all the "peon" employees there to assist him. Finally, the new ticket was issued along with the boarding pass and I was ready to continue the flight to my final destination of Recife.

Then the unexpected, or perhaps the expected, occurred. I could only assume that Varig had been doing this route for months if not years, that everyone knew "the drill," and not to what would just happen. The huge Boeing 707 continuing its route to I do not know where, perhaps the return flight to Miami, started the four engines, revved them up, and backed out of its spot in front of the passenger terminal. But then it turned, still in reverse, with all four thrusters facing the front of the terminal. The four engines now at full blast hit the large plate glass windows of the terminal directly in front of the airline counter where I was standing and suddenly shattered them all. Huge pieces of glass were flying through the air and without time to think, I sat down on my haunches behind the ticket counter (like a good northeasterner from the interior of Pernambuco), thus avoiding the glass flying overhead. I was luckily unscathed from the flying sheets of glass and somehow saw no others injured. In fact, all seemed to be quite normal; the plane taxied away from the terminal, no one said anything more.

I had arrived in Brazil.

4

RETURN TO RECIFE – EVERYTHING IS NOT AS IT SEEMS

On the continuing flight, there was a familiar figure at the gate after we walked across that steaming tarmac at Guararapes Airport in Recife, none other than old acquaintance Geroaldo Captain of Police and of the Pernambuco office of the DOPS [Department of Public Security]. He had a big smile on his face, gave me that one-half embrace of Brazilian men greeting each other, one hand on shoulder, the other in a firm hand shake and said "Oi, Gaherty! De novo em nossa terra!" I said something inane like "Hey Geroaldo, you haven't changed a bit, still that 'cool' Brazilian!" He went on like we were old friends, "This time all is different; bygones will be bygones. That last unfortunate incident in 1967 outside the "Bar Acadêmico" and you being hauled off to detention with all the lousy leftists was just that – unfortunate. I apologize for your getting roughed up, but hey, it turned out all right with your INR buddy bailing you out. But now we are totally apprised of the situation and are happy you will be an official reporter for the "Times" and INR-WHA since our DOPS has good relations with them. We're checked back on your last visit and the reporting of that "Cordel" poem on the bombing at Guararapes Airport and the terrorist attempt on (now) President Costa e Silva's life and especially the one from Paraiba filling the peasants' heads with lies and shit from Cuban propaganda, "Letter to Mr. Kennedy;" both were a big help in keeping abreast of mass sentiment in the interior. We understand you will continue this line of reporting, and more important, thinking.

I just want you to know you are in good hands; we'll be keeping an eye out for you and on you."

With that in mind I took a taxi back to the old area near the Chácara das Rosas [The "Rose House"] near Avenida da Boa Vista and the Law School of Pernambuco and the "pé sujo" [o Bar Acadêmico] where all hell had broken loose in 1967. The city in 1969, two years after my initial research of 1966-1967, was in a growth rhythm, lots of new construction including tall buildings on the side of the Capibaribe River in downtown, but one could still see much poverty along the streets of the city. There was more traffic on the large arteries of the City Center; people were still walking across the many bridges and ragged beggars were to be seen, some with bandaged wounds on their swollen legs. I was overwhelmed by the increase in traffic and the resulting barrage of noise in the streets, some of them yet the old colonial cobblestone ["paralelepípedo"]. Rush hour was now part of old Recife, in the morning movement to work, at mid-day for those still driving home for the big mid - day meal, and in the afternoon or early evening when the sound of engines, blowing horns and exhaust smoke filled the air.

My old hangout to rest and have fun with friends, Boa Viagem Beach, was different with new skyscrapers, new hotels and tall apartment buildings. The young girls now wore bikinis instead of the old one-piece "maillot" of just two years past, the sign of both small and great changes since 1967. The ubiquitous soccer games were still scattered all along the beach of Boa Viagem and to the north toward Pina; I wondered if this was due to the unemployment that still was the norm for the poor boys and young men of Pina.

I lived in a "Republic" of college age students in the Brazilian substitute for college dorms: several fellows in a "boarding apartment" often run by a widow needing the income. This was thanks to good friend Pedro Oliveira of the old days in Recife. It was on a high floor of a tall apartment building near the old Law School of Pernambuco whose library was much frequented by me in the 1966-1967 research time. The colorful boarding house, "The Rose House" or "Chácara das Rosas" of the earlier time, sitting on prime real estate, had been demolished and a tall, shiny apartment building was going up in its place. If not a step in financial gain for the perhaps opportunistic or more likely, greedy owners, then it certainly represented a loss of "character" for the neighborhood. The "Chácara" was well-known in those parts. (My God, my Spanish Golden Age Poetry studies have enabled me to inadvertently use a "Gongorismo" figure of speech: "if not … then.")

Living conditions were a lot better than in 1966 both regarding comfort, hygiene of the bathrooms and in the food. The "Dona" prepared a mid-day meal of rice, beans, a portion of beef, tomatoes, onion and with a "cafezinho" and a slice of guava jam for dessert. The evening meal might be fried eggs, tomatoes, onion, French bread, bean soup, banana, and "café com leite."

Shortly after arriving in Recife, I went to my old spot ["ponto"] for research, the São José Market in old Recife, in search of "Literatura de Cordel" at the old poetry stand of Edson Pinto. I noted that I spied only one "cordel" vendor in the entire market, a substantial change from 1966. I would soon find that political change and the escalating war between soldiers and students had changed things even for the humble booklets of "Cordel," politics becoming a "dangerous plate" (referring to the daily blue-plate lunch special in Brazil) according to one of the major poets still writing in the Northeast.

During that June of 1969 I and friends enjoyed the festivities of St. John's Day in Camarigipe, a beautiful celebration and not dangerous at all. There were two bands, one of northeastern country ["caipira"] music and one of Brazilian rock and roll of the times ["a música iê-iê-iê"], fireworks and beautiful northeastern "square dancing" ["quadrilhas"]. It all reminded me of Jorge Amado's descriptions of the same festival in his novels on the cacao zone in Bahia.

There were articles in the newspapers each day complaining of the none too appealing Brazilian economic situation. The year of 1969 was particularly one of crisis: high inflation, fear of "Yankee Imperialism" controlling Brazil, cries for a higher minimum wage, and the lack of money in peoples' pockets and even in the coffers of the government with one result being bringing to a halt the local efforts in public and social works trying to ameliorate the situation of the chronic droughts in the Northeast.

All the above, so far, went into that first "Letter" of 1969 to the "Times" with a copy to INR.

A cultural note for the casual readers interested in folklore (anything related to the "Cordel" and northeastern culture was a "command performance" for me): I saw the film "Maria Bonita Queen of the Bandits" ["Maria Bonita, Rainha do Cangaço"], a totally romanticized version of the story, only slightly based on the life of Lampião and his consort. It was newer and in color, but with the same romanticism of the classic "Bandit" ["O Cangaceiro"] made years earlier by Lima Barreto. The former films, like "Stream of Blood" ["Riacho de Sangue"], were in stark contrast to the films with northeastern themes so important to the New Cinema ["Cinema Novo"] of directors like Glauber Rocha of the late 1960s. "God and the Devil in the Land of the Sun" ["Deus e o Diabo na Terra do Sol"] is an excellent example of the latter. Only a coincidence, but maybe not much, were the Italian "Spaghetti Westerns" of similar days like Clint Eastwood in "The Good, the Bad and the Ugly."

Another sign of the times: the paranoia from the Right, the fear of Communism, communists and "subversives" had grown exponentially in those two years. With the fear came the government repression, now a constant in life in Brazil. The much beloved music of the MPB ["Música Popular Brasileira"] linked to the annual festivals televised nationally with the nation's love affair with Chico Buarque de Hollanda, Geraldo Vandré, Nara Leão, the young Caetano Veloso, Milton Nascimento, Jair Rodrígues and others had taken another direction. Samba still reigned but Chico was in "voluntary" exile in Italy, Nara Leão also in Europe, Caetano Veloso was in England, and the star of Jair Rodrigues was ebbing. Most important was the absence of Geraldo Vandré and the Festival of 1967 with his "anthem" – "Disparada," the singer-composer either disappeared or dead. So, what was left? Roberto Carlos the King of Brazilian Rock and the "iê-iê-iê" and the "western" singers imitating United States' country music ("os sereteiros"). And "forró" was coming into its own. Music was to entertain and not comment on society. The one good thing of all this is that the censorship and repression would lead to arguably the most creative Brazilian popular music of all time with the satire, double-entendre and witticisms of those heroes of MPB who managed to oppose the dictatorship in their limited ways, mainly "driblando a censura" ["fooling the censorship"].

I would go often to the movies in Recife that "winter" mostly with buddies from the boarding house. We noticed some changes from 1967. The political climate of the times was visible across the nation, always present in the movie previews ("trailers") dealing with the activities of the military always in the rhythm of "economic development" and the "March to the West." Economic Minister Roberto Campos and more importantly the Minister of the Interior Delfim Neto would come under fire, the latter seemingly growing fatter as time passed by, the dictatorship going on, all this time with the promised "slice of the big cake" never delivered to the masses. In the "trailer" movie preview, when yet another ribbon was cut by a general or admiral revealing yet another statue of military heroes, when there had been whistling, catcalls, jokes and even booing and jeering two year ago, now there was utter silence in the movie theater. A deafening silence.

Well, I should say, silence most of the time. On one occasion Pedro Oliveira, my old buddy from the boarding house, could not resist and whistled and hissed when one more ribbon was cut. More than once in that darkened theater on Boa Vista I thought I spotted the same person sitting just a few rows behind us, innocuous but for the black tie and white linen suit, not usual movie attending attire. I said to good buddy Pedro, "Don't look now, but check out that guy four rows behind us. He has been in the same spot the last time or two we were here." Walking out of the theater, we were stopped by Geroaldo the same guy at the airport in June when I arrived, who flashed a badge and said, "Gaherty, your friend here should learn to keep his mouth shut and be more of a patriot. Be careful who you hang out with. Consider this my first warning to both of you." Slightly stunned, I stammered, "Fine. I'll tell Pedro to tone it down a bit. He meant no harm. Maybe we can come late and just see the feature." The cop or agent retorted, "Yeah, that sounds like a good plan, and besides it would be hard to whistle or hiss with a broken jaw."

A bit lighter entertainment was available and had not changed: the visits and nightlife to Boa Viagem Beach and the red-light zone for fun times. I usually went with the same buddy as to the movies, Pedro Oliveira, who by the way, had survived the DOPS' surveillance from that tear gas police episode in 1967; Pedro in fact had helped me get the new "digs" in the boarding house in that high-rise in Boa Vista. We would go back to Boa Viagem and the zone to try to relive those good times from 1966 and 1967 (including the best night of folkloric music I ever experienced in Brazil, an after-hours time with a whorehouse band). After my last experience with the clap and a huge dose of tetracycline which led to a goddam hemorrhoidectomy in Lincoln, I wasn't quite so adventurous. When the sexy, cute lady of the night invited me to do a "69," saying "That's my favorite," I said, "How about just a quick screw and we'll call it even?" There was still no mention of a condom, so dumb Gaherty might have had a repeat of 1967. It turned out okay.

Many other things had not changed in the day to day "normal" in Recife, moments that caught the "gringo's" attention in the Northeast and good fodder for the new "Letters." One evening I was seated on a stool at the counter of a café near Guararapes Avenue just eating a sandwich. I felt or perhaps just sensed some movement behind me, turned around, and about three inches from my rear end was the headlight and bumper of a Volkswagen "Bug." Keep in mind this is between the lunch counter and the wall just a few feet away. It turns out that was the best place for the owner to park his car each night. I knew street parking space was at a premium but didn't figure it would interrupt a snack.

There are many bridges linking the mainland to the peninsula, the peninsula to the island all in greater downtown Recife with the three rivers that run through it, and as mentioned earlier, many of the bridges yet in 1969 were "spots" for beggars, some with their swollen legs wrapped in bandages. And there was talk of Schistomiasis, a disease still present in the Northeast in those times, a fact verified by several of my United States Peace Corps Volunteer friends. The disease came from a parasite in the form of a worm, in its early form a type of snail, which grew in the intestines of its victims, the worm being found in the stagnant waters of ponds and small lakes and even the rivers of the interior. The worm can be up to one meter in length! The symptoms are stomach pains, blood and horrible damage to the liver. Just a thought – is this why so many northeasterners in the 1960s were all taking prescribed medicines ("remédios") for their liver? Even the young college guys seemed to be on the medicine. And of course, totally unrelated, but a "must" reference to Brazilian Literature is the great Monteiro Lobato's short story "O Fígado Indiscreto" ["The Indiscrete Liver"] the story of a young man betrothed to a fine young lady and his "engagement" dinner at the family home when he was served, yes, a huge slab of liver. He of course had an aversion to the same, in fact detested it, and the rest of this hilarious story is how he attempted to avoid eating it and at the same time not offending his perhaps future mother-in-law. I can say no more; please look up the story and read it.

Another moment took place at the Second-Hand Bookstore in Recife. The store is famous; I met its owner Mr. Gomes in 1966 when I was searching out and buying so many "classics" of northeastern folklore which were only available through him (and the "Livraria São José" in Rio de Janeiro). Anyway, we met again in 1969 in Recife. In those years of the late 1960s Gomes was in his heyday – a "Golden Age" of "blank check" sales to major United States Universities greedy to get the best of Brazilian books for their libraries in a sort of "book race" (read "space race") for predominance in the field. The University of Texas comes to mind. Gomes informed me that there was a new national law in place in Brazil: at the death of a writer, artist, or intellectual, the individual's library (and these people were true bibliophiles!) had to remain intact in Brazil. The collections could not be sold and taken out of the country. The activities of booksellers like Gomes were considered by a large portion of Brazilians to be another type of capitalist exploitation by the United States of poor, third world countries. The bookseller told me he had already been accused of selling "rarities" to the United States. This is but a small "vignette" of the anti-United States views from the left in Brazil at the time; it existed side by side with the right-wing paranoia already described.

On the research trips in 1966, 1967, and now in 1969 while in Recife I depended on the post office for correspondence with my family at home in the U.S. I received my mail in the building of USIS (United States Information Service) and it involved a long walk from the boarding house near Boa Vista Avenue and Guararapes Avenue in City Center to the island where USIS was located. On the return, always with letters from home in Lincoln, Nebraska, I would stop in an open air café on Avenida Guararapes, buy a "Time" Magazine in English to "cure my homesickness" ("matar saudades" as they say in Portuguese), and drink an icy "Guaraná" or perhaps a "Brahma Choppe" beer while I read the letters from home, or from my girlfriend Molly in D.C.

Sending letters home was another story. A citizen of the United States was not prepared to deal with the "battle" that would take place in the post office. Allow me to explain. First of all, one encountered all the commerce going on outside the building on the post office steps; it all seemed like a bazaar in Istanbul! Vendors were selling oranges, bananas, "cafezinhos" from thermos bottles, cigarettes and boxes of wooden matches and of course writing paper, envelopes and BIC pens. The local custom for many was to buy the writing materials, write the letter on the spot, and then go into the Post Office to mail it.

An Aside. I cannot help but smile thinking of the BIC pens. Any student of Brazilian Literature must remember Luís Fernando Veríssimo and his "chronicles" of those years and in particular the stories of that very Brazilian creation – the detective Ed Morte. An unsuccessful Brazilian version of "Guy Noir" of Lake Wobegon Fame or even a take - off on Mickey Spillane, Ed worked out of a tiny cubicle in São Paulo, the office populated by the cockroaches and mice scurrying about. And on at least one occasion Ed had to pawn his "BIC collection" to get the local paper.

It turns out the envelopes and even the stamps you bought after waiting in long lines did not have glue on them. The "jeito" ["deal"] was to buy said envelope and stamp and then go to a tiny, round table in the middle of the big room where there were small glue pots with tiny brushes in them. For a person who can play classical guitar, other tasks needing dexterity were a challenge to me (like wrapping Christmas presents – the "job from hell" would be as Christmas package wrapper in Macy's). So I ended up with a mess: glue all over the outside of the envelope, wet stamps with too much glue, and worse, glue all over my fingers, hands and the shirt I wore that day.

But then the next "adventure" began. With envelope sealed and stamped, one gets in line to send the letter "regular" mail, or "register" the letter, or perhaps "registered air mail," each requiring a separate line. The Brazilians did not seem to mind the long wait, all loudly conversing with much laughter. Not so the "gringo" accustomed to just an air mail stamp and dropping the letter in the proper post office box. I knew no Brazilian that even minutely believed that a letter sent by "regular mail" would ever arrive at its destination. But I noticed something funny: behind each steel "guiché" or cage where the employees sat there was a huge pile of letters, all casually tossed there from the respective cage. Did the Post Office ever separate the different letters from that huge pile? Did each have the same fate?

The post office employees were notoriously badly paid, and it was no surprise to observe their usual bad humor ("casmurros" or ill-humored, a term taken from the famous novel by the great 19th century Brazilian novelist Machado de Assis: "Dom Casmurro") and then have to deal with it. I would customarily greet said employee with great courtesy: "How are you today? I hope all goes well for you and your family" and hope for the best.

5

ARIANO SUASSUNA AND
"PUBLISH OR PERISH"

It was in those days in the headlines of the "Diário de Pernambuco" I read of my mentor and guide to Northeastern culture, Ariano Suassuna (his "The Rogues' Trial" – "Auto da Compadecida" – had been one of the chapters of my Ph.D. dissertation, this because it was the Brazilian work that most used the "literatura de cordel"). On a visit to Ariano's house and our first reunion since 1967, I learned that the "Auto" had been made into a commercial film and in these days was awaiting its "premiere" in the Brazilian cinema. Ariano said, "There is only one problem: the government censors in Brasília are not ready to "liberate" the film. They say I have to travel to Brasília and defend the text and the film!" All was eventually resolved. The doubts of the government had to do with the author's comments in his text as to bureaucracy and corruption in the Brazilian government (one should recall that Suassuna wrote and produced the play in 1955, years before the "Redeemer" Revolution of 1964!) Also, it was being bandied about that the cause of the censorship was the fact that the author chose to place a black Jesus Christ in the cast, a fact that he attributed to "American Racism!" This was just one more of the many signs of political change and the political climate that I would see in 1969. The paranoid government of the generals saw the "leftist subversion" everywhere, even in the text of this so innocent and so northeastern folk drama! The irony of the moment came later: once released, the film broke all attendance records up to that time for Brazilian Cinema.

I might add that after getting off the bus back at Conde de Boa Vista and walking back to the boarding house, Geroaldo himself, one of the "mucky-mucks" of the local DOPS, pulled up beside me on the sidewalk and leaning on the fender of a big black sedan issued a friendly wave for me to stop and said, "Mike, good to see you again. We have an eye on Suassuna and the business of that subversive film. Just be sure you remember whose side you are on." He slapped me on the back, winked and got back in the car.

I might be on the alert for events and personages in Brazil (like Ariano) for "Letters" to the "Times," but there was that pesky "other thing" – publishing part or all the dissertation in Brazil. In that vein there were several days and encounters with the folks at the "Instituto Joaquim Nabuco de Pesquisas Sociais" [Joaquim Nabuco Instiutute of Social Scienes] in the "Casa Forte" district of western Recife. I had done serious research there in 1966, perusing classic works on Brazilian folklore and checking out the "Cordel" collection. It was there I fell asleep in a Gilberto Freyre lecture after the big mid-day meal (unheard of and a "Mortal Sin" in Recife), and where I waxed enthusiastic hearing the wonderful lectures of Brazil's most famous folklorist Luís da Câmara Cascudo (I would travel to Natal to have a private session with him.) So, in 1969 I arrived with manuscript in hand, offering a text based on my Ph.D. thesis of 1968 for publication. There were courteous chats with the "masters" of the Institute – Sylvio Rabelo, Mauro Mota, and Renato Carneiro Campos. The latter took some interest in the text and drove me out to the "Casa Grande" to see the famous founder of the JNIPS Gilberto Freyre. The entire endeavor of the research institute was founded in part on the fact Freyre was a descendant of the sugar cane aristocracy of the Northeast, had a large hunk of property on one of the old sugar cane mill "fazendas" ["plantations] which he would convert into the modern Institute, incidentally named after a major Northeastern intellectual of the 19th century, Joaquim Nabuco. He was also parlaying his prestige as a federal congressman, this in turn reflecting his intellectual fame – author of "Casa Grande e Senzala" ["The Masters and the Slaves"] a classic of Brazilian history and sociology, incidentally the off-shoot of his M.A. Thesis at Columbia University in New York. He was as we say in the old days in the Northeast the "manda-chuva" or even the "bamba do bairro" - the "big cheese" making it all go! A "yes" by the master and my manuscript would magically appear in print. He indeed agreed that it would, at least in part, be a nice article in the review of the Institute. And it did not hurt for my INR connection that Freyre was from the old aristocracy, pro-military and "in with Flynn" in the new regime.

But I was after "bigger fish" and that brought Ariano Sussuna back into the picture. That all happened shortly after the Joaquim Nabuco business. On yet another visit to Ariano's office (he was head of the "Department of Extension and Culture" for the state of Pernambuco) that June, the motive this time was to "pave the way" for a favor from him – to read part of my dissertation and discuss avenues of possible publication in Recife. I showed him the entire manuscript; he saw it as a small monograph or book to be published by the University Press of the "Universidade Federal de Pernambuco." At any rate, he accompanied me in a chauffeured car of "The Department of Extension and Culture" one fine day that June to the University Press, introduced me to the director, and it was a "done deal". Ariano being my "guide" in the whole matter. After a brief chat with the director (who knew who he was talking to) Ariano said to me, "All set. You are the boss and your wish is my command." Or something to that effect. He said he himself would take care of the revision of the text and the book should come out in August of 1969, just two months later. Nossa! As they would say in Brazil in those days, "Great" in English. I breathed a tremendous sigh of relief; the major purpose of that summer's research was done and "in the bag."

Before I get on with what happened afterwards, I must finish what I was going to say, something important for the "Times" readers, a real vignette of what life in northeastern Brazil and the life of one of its great literary icons was like – tradition in architecture and style in Recife! Ariano's house told the whole story. The house was in the colonial style, surrounded by walls and a large steel entry gate. It was replete with gardens with all kinds of tropical plants and flowers. The outside front of the house was ablaze with the blue tiles ["azulejos"] inherited from the Portuguese and Arabic Traditions in Portugal. Inside there were high ceilings, all the rooms open to the air. (Hey, we are in tropical Brazil!) The furniture was all in the colonial style, mostly of Brazilian rosewood or "Jacarandá" in the form of no less than four rocking chairs and two benches, all "caned" in the style of the tropical Northeast and its colonial heritage. The living room was a true museum of northeastern art, painted portraits of the Baptism of Jesus, at least one done by Ariano himself, and yet others by Fransisco Brennand and Samico (friends of Suassuana, the former now attracting hundreds of thousands of dollars for his works and Samico not far behind). They were all colleagues in that great effervescence of northeastern cultural life in the late 1940s and 1950s, a real Renaissance of art in the region. There was a statue of St. George (São Jorge) in the corner, impossible to leave out! And the floor was of northeastern tiles without any carpeting. There were other paintings, evidence of Ariano's project, the "Romance da Pedra do Reino" ["Romance of the Rock of the Kingdom"] and the important intellectual-artistic movement initiated by Ariano, the "Movimento Armorial" ["Armorial Movement"]. A minor note, but interesting for the North American was the use of mosquito netting in all the bedrooms, recalling the "muriçocas" or mosquitoes of the "Rose House" in Recife in 1966 and 1967.

Related to the government censorship of the "Auto" earlier that winter in Recife was yet another facet of Ariano's personality or even philosophy as a writer and intellectual. He said to me on one of those occasions in 1969 that he would do anything to avoid travel to Rio, São Paulo or even Brasília preferring the image of the "intellectual of the provinces" (he was in good company – Brazil's most important folklorist Luís da Câmara Casudo, adopted the same stance). But time passed, the times changed, and Ariano would have to make an exception to the rule for no less than the occasion of being accepted into the august company of the "acadêmicos" in the Brazilian Academy of Letters in Rio de Janeiro. A subsequent moment, of much greater national exposure, was when one of the Samba Schools of Rio chose as their theme "Ariano Suassuna" and our humble servant somehow acquiesced to ride on the float in the huge carnival parade in Rio. This means, in the Brazilian parlance, "You have arrived!" To put it all in perspective, singer-song writer, novelist, social protestor "par excellence" Chico Buarque received the same honor in those times.

Relieved, it was time to get on with other business, checking out "Cordel" in the São José Market and life in Recife. Time to have some fun as well. There was a lot of beer drinking at the old "Academic Bar" across from the Pernambuco Law School (the scene of that scary, near calamity of 1967 detailed in "Letters I"). My main friends were still from that time, especially Pedro Oliveira, and Fábio Heráclio whose father was the retired Admiral from the Brazilian Navy and had sugar cane plantation connections. Pedro and I lived, as I said, in that student "Republic" or boarding house still near the bar. Later that month I and some student friends in the "Republic" in Recife were celebrating Pedro's birthday in the apartment in the boarding house and all with great enthusiasm. Someone, as a joke, shouted "Viva Cuba!" Just a few short minutes later there was a loud knocking on the door; it was the police wanting to know what was going on and threatening to haul us all down to the city jail. Only after much conversation did we convince the sincere police officer that it was all a joke, but the year 1969 was not much of a joke for Brazilians. The officer took names and it got back to Geroaldo, but I only found out about that later.

As proof of the atmosphere of those days there were newspaper articles each day about the threats to the "Red Bishop," Dom Hêlder Câmara of the Arch Diocese of Recife as well as news of the assassination of a Catholic priest in the city. Once more, the paranoia of the Right, the fear of communism, of the Left and of the "subversives" was augmented in the city. It was precisely in 1969 that a serious note came out in the newspapers of Recife. The house of the "Red Bishop" was machine gunned, the bullets scarring the front of the episcopal house, and the bishop threatened with death. In those same days Father Mello was assassinated in the Jesuit University, a message to the "Progressive Church" and to the clergy leaning toward Liberation Theology to not speak or take any action unfavorable to the military regime.

A personal aside from a moment later that Pernambuco winter when I was ready to leave Recife and move down to Rio: while waiting for a flight in the "Aeroporto dos Guararapes" in Recife when I saw from a distance this short little fellow in clerical garb, with a leather briefcase in one hand, and I said to myself: "It's him! Dom Hêlder Câmara!" I stammered a stupid question, "Sir, are you Dom Hêlder Câmara?" The short northeasterner smiled and said, "No, I'm his brother." Then, after the joke, we had an altogether too short conversation but one unforgettable for me. I shall never forget the "Red Bishop's" mantra: "The greatest violence on the planet is hunger."

On my way to the São José Market to check out any new story-poems at Edson Pinto's poetry stand, I would often go by the Post Office to mail letters home. (I have told the story of post office adventures with the glue pots, sticky sleeves, hands and fingers a mess and letters covered with glue earlier on.) It was on one of those occasions I witnessed the "arm of the law" but not in a sinister political sense, just day to day living in the Northeast, yet important for the next "Letter" to New York. In those years it was common to see on the streets of downtown Recife all manner of "semi-legal" commerce. It was illegal to sell anything on the city streets without a license. Just the same the streets were filled with the "illegal" vendors especially near the Post Office. In a feeble attempt to stop the street selling, the city employed a large open bed truck circulating on the streets with the ostensible purpose of catching the vendors "red handed," confiscating their goods and who knows what fate if they actually caught the vendors.

On that occasion Avenida Guararapes was jammed with traffic, cars and buses belching smoke, and the normal mass of humanity in the streets. Suddenly outside the steps of the Post Office all the vendors were yelling at each other and waving madly, giving the sign that the "fuzz" ["o rapa"] was coming down the street, that is, that big lumbering truck of the city. One poor little vendor tried to pick up his wooden stand filled with limes, trying to hide it behind a post at the Post Office, and it all went splattering wildly in the street, limes in all directions and the vendor in another, and he shouting the whole time warning his buddies of the "rapa." Suddenly there was a wild scene with all the street vendors running in all directions, all shouting to each other, and hiding behind columns and posts of buildings and the post office itself. The crowd in the streets, witnessing the scene, all yelled and rooted for the vendors. One of the latter ran in front of the city truck, crossed the bridge on the river, and a few minutes later returned to his hiding place behind a column of the post office, a broad "shit eating" grin on his face the whole time.

It was all a bit ironic since the "contraband" they sold consisted in some limes, oranges, bananas, and let's face it, some BIC ink pens (used by the folks entering the Post Office to write last minute letters to be mailed that day). I was thinking that there ought to have been more important matters to concern the Military Police and the City than to harass street vendors, but evidently the "legitimate" businesses along Guararapes felt threatened by the hordes of street vendors in front of their shops and complained to the "fuzz." However, it was the horde of street vendors hawking all manner of wares, even shouting their wares with the age-old Pernambuco tradition of the "pregões" that made for a colorful life in Recife yet in those days. If one kept his eyes open, there was no end of surprises and I was happy to report the same as a cultural vignette to the "Times."

And yet another "small" moment reflecting life in the hot tropics of Recife appeared shortly on the back pages of the newspaper; it was an article about the small time, young thugs at the open-air food market in Olinda, up on the hill from Recife. There are young boys who work at the market offering to carry home the groceries or other purchases, most often in small wagons or carts. Evidently the thugs offer "protection" and want "protection money" to leave the young boys alone. No money and you get a whipping! Despicable! The tiny article caught my attention because of my research in Salvador da Bahia on the famous "Cordel" poet Rodolfo Coelho Cavalcante who was one of the most prolific poets of all times with perhaps 1,700 booklets of narrative poetry. He did the same job as a child – carrying goods from the market - "fretando na feira" in his home town in Alagoas State. I was thinking New York readers of the "Times" might be familiar with the protection racket from that mafia underworld in the city and might relate to the modest northeastern version.

6

A RETURN TO "JUBIABÁ" – BLAME IT ON JORGE AMADO

The reporting for "Letters" so far was pretty much day to day, no earth-shaking events yet, but I still had a penchant for troubles. I always had that curiosity about Brazil and Brazilians that was insatiable, maybe a trait of a good researcher and/or journalist, and it got the DOPS' interest one incredibly hot day that summer. I dedicate this moment to the student of Brazilian Literature with a knowledge of the works of the master Jorge Amado. Friend Fábio Heráclio from 1967 days, now a full-fledged electrical engineer and with a new VW "Fusca" ["Bug"] was showing me around Recife. We went to the main docks in the old port of Recife one morning and this scene awaited us: there was a huge cargo ship docked, the holds opened in wide spaces, stacks and stacks of boxes and sacks in view. On the dock there were dozens of men, mostly black, all dressed in ragged t-shirts and shorts and sandals or flip-flops, all sweating profusely in that tropical sun of Recife, moving the sacks and boxes from the cranes to the beds of long travel trailers and semi - trucks. They used a sort of gunny sack over the head and shoulder for their only "tool." The sacks were all labeled: "Donated by the People of the United States of America." It was dried food from the Alliance for Progress of the times in Brazil. This of course was a carryover from the regime of John F. Kennedy and the swell of a new alliance with Latin America and a period of increase in friendly relations, notwithstanding Cuba and the Bay of Pigs. But now, years later, the enthusiasm was ebbing, and even though Brazil's military government was receiving aid from the U.S., the masses, particularly the masses of the northeast distrusted the U.S. and thought of it all as another part of "Yankee imperialism". They considered the food donations a disaster, believing that most ended up sold by thieves, and that it would be far better to send machines, like road building equipment. (I wrote of that phase of the Alliance in "LETTERS" in 1966; see the story of the rusting bulldozers, tractors and heavy road building equipment at the docks of Natal, donations from the United States "buried" in Brazilian bureaucracy and corruption of the times.)

In another part of the dock it was a true scene from Jorge Amado's "Jubiabá" and its stevedore hero turned boxer Balduíno: large ships carrying raw sugar from Brazil and many black stevedores loading the heavy sacks weighing 80 kilos each onto the ships. The sugar was brought by many large trucks to the docks from the sugar cane mills and refineries of the northeast interior, all waiting in lines to be unloaded. I noted that it was not the white refined sugar we see in supermarkets and dinner tables at home in Nebraska, but the brown, "raw" sugar in use in Brazil. The many stevedores were dressed in rags, mostly black men but some mixed, both mulatto and "caboclo" (Indian-White) mixtures from the Northeast. I had snapped a few photos of both scenes, the Food for Peace and the sugar cane loading.

I thought nothing about it, but as we got back in Fábio's "VW bug," a black sedan (I was getting used to the "company" car by now) cut us off, and Geroaldo of the DOPS got out of the back seat, dressed in his usual white linen suit and hat and black necktie. He walked up to the window on my side and said, "Why don't you and your buddy get out of the car, and we'll walk over to the shade by the warehouse and have a talk?" Fábio, always a bit quick on the trigger and from that old upper-class aristocracy, was not about to take any bullshit, and said (loose translation) "Who the f*** are you? Do you know who in the hell you are screwing around with?" Geroaldo, unperturbed, said, "I think it's you who might want to be a little careful with that foul mouth of yours. I'm Geroaldo Captain of Police and local DOPS in Recife, and I'm not used to any shithead of a young punk ordering me around." (I noticed a burly driver had gotten out of Geroaldo's car and was moving slowly toward us.) In case you and friend Mike here did not notice, there was a warning sign at the entrance to the dock and these ships for authorized personnel only. I assume your fancy upper class education included reading and writing, so you better have an explanation." Fábio said, "None needed asshole. Show me your badge and I'll take it up with the governor when I see him tomorrow."

Suddenly the burly guy rushed up, slammed us both against the wall, said, "drop the pants and hands on the wall!" (This was standard police routine when confronting bank robbers on the streets in Brazil). Fábio tried to take a swing at him and got his face slammed against the bricks. Bleeding from below the eye and nose, and wiping his face with a handkerchief, he was smart enough to stay quiet at least for the moment. Geroaldo, getting hot and more impatient in that sun, said, "The governor knows we are taking enough shit from Miguel Arraes, Francisco Julião and the Left for that Alliance for Progress Food being unloaded and carted off in those semis and wants no snooping around by anybody, and that includes you and of course our "investigative journalist – researcher" Mr. Gaherty. So why don't you just go on home, put some band aids on your face and when you talk to the governor tomorrow, I suspect you'll see this was all under orders and on the up and up and it would be a good thing to just forget it ever happened. Gaherty, on the other hand, I would not put this in the 'Letter' to Hansen or Iverson. There might be a few too many questions asked when you mention the Alliance. Let's let well enough alone; the USA is doing us a big favor with all the excess dried milk, flour and such and the Brazilian people surely appreciate it. Go on and get the hell out of here; we'll be in touch."

Fábio's bleeding had subsided and he was alert if not calmed down enough to follow orders. He started the car and speeded out of the dock area and then we drove rapidly to the Heráclio house. He immediately got on the phone to his father the retired Admiral from the Brazilian Navy and jabbered what had happened, all in a Portuguese about ten times too fast for me to get. We drank a couple of Brahma choppe beers while Fábio explained his Dad was putting in a call to the governor's office and we would have an answer in a few minutes. When the phone rang, Fábio picking it up, alternating between protesting in language I had never heard him use, and then silence, he hung up and turned to me, "Merda. It's true. The governor does have a hush-hush policy on the goings on at the docks and wants absolutely no complications. He said he was sorry for this unfortunate incident involving an Admiral's son and his good American friend. He said he would 'settle' with the DOPS agent and his bodyguard, and we should forget the entire unfortunate incident." I was aware Fábio carried a pistol in the glove compartment of the car and was glad he did not have a chance to get it out. This was an all too real incident of that extreme Northeastern machismo on both parts – the cops and my friend. In the old days, a hired bandit would settle matters in cold blood, and even now there would possibly be some consequences. Merda! All because I wanted to see the docks and what went on there.

Just a few days later an opposite scene would take place. It was a historic moment: The United States' astronauts landing on the moon! It was all televised, but on the black and white screens of TV in the Northeast. I saw the entire scene on a TV in an ice cream shop on a street corner in Recife near the Law School. Friends from my boarding apartment and many others whom I did not know rushed up to me, offering big embraces ("abraços") or shaking hands, congratulating me on the event, as though I had something to do with it! The next day there would be story-poems from "Cordel" selling like hot cakes in the city markets and downtown street corners, notably in the coming days three different editions by the poet-singer José Soares known as the "Poet Reporter of "Cordel" in Recife. He was known for "scooping" the major dailies upon occasion with his quick journalistic style booklets of verse.

Of the several story-poems on the Recife scene I noted the different approaches taken by the poets: one with perhaps the very detailed operations of the landing itself, but also curiously others with major emphasis given to the food the astronauts ate and how they ate it. Perhaps significant or not in a "hungry" northeast interior and peasants who bought "Cordel," these details in some stories had more pages dedicated to them than the feat itself. And one should note that yet in the late 1960s everyone in the Northeast was aware of the "Space Race" between the United States and the Soviet Union, of "Sputnik" and the Russian success a year or two before, and the failure just days before the U.S. moon landing of the Russian attempt on the moon. Many skeptical, humble northeasterners in the interior still believed the whole thing was a "set up," a cinematic "creation" by the U.S. and not the real thing. The Cold War, fear once again of U.S. imperialism, the case of Cuba, Fidel and Ché Guevara, all figured in this atmosphere. But for me that day in Pernambuco, it was good to be an American! Such stories were great text for both Hansen and the "Times" and Iverson and the INR, always looking to see how the "Cordel" reflected local sentiment among the northeastern masses. For that matter the DOPS and Geroaldo would be beaming – anything favoring the U.S. (and the alliance with Brazil's military) and anti-Soviet Union was great. One of Geroaldo's guys came out of the ice cream store eating a huge cocoanut ice cream (Brazilian style, with a small plastic spoon and not licking it as an American would). He sidled up to me, gave that half one-arm embrace and said, "Gaherty, viva América".

The truth is not much else was going on with "Cordel" to report; we were entering "full repression" in the middle of 1969 and the poets were smart enough to not make waves (once again quoting the Pernambuco poet who said "politics is a dangerous plate right now"). I had visited Edson Pinto's "Cordel" stand in the São José market for many weeks and discovered little new was coming out, at least in a social or political vein. I've written of the paranoia, the "para-military" threats to the Catholic clergy. I had the big success with Ariano and the promise to publish my dissertation, so frankly, little remained to do in Recife other than the partying in Boa Viagem and a couple of ersatz moments when I played some vintage U.S. rock n' roll in the local night clubs.

7

FLYING DOWN TO RIO

So, I headed on down to Rio with some excitement and enthusiasm but also trepidation – Cristina Maria awaited! There was some unfinished business and a few surprises in store. She had after all introduced me to the music of Chico Buarque de Hollanda and now he and others were faced with the evolution of AI-5 - the "prior censorship" and attack on intellectuals, writers and especially the MPB composers.

On my limited budget from the beginning in 1966 and yet on this trip in 1969 I depended on the bus system, and it had changed drastically since 1967. Before, on the sign in the center above the windshield of each bus one would see the destination of the bus: i.e. Downtown, Botafogo, Maracanã, etc. And below, in the right-hand corner, a placard would show the route to the destination: "Downtown via Jardim Botânico" for example. Now the placard above has only a number, i.e. 420, 325 or the like, and no one knows the relation of the number to the actual destination. There is mass confusion. With the passage of time eventually it did all get sorted out and the public learned the relationship between the number and the destination. Supposedly there was a guidebook with all this pertinent information available at the time, but I met no one that had such a book. After several rides, including getting lost more than once in Rio, I gradually was able to learn how to get around. The good news is I got to know a lot of Rio I had not counted on knowing!

Along with the bus changes there were major traffic changes in Rio. The city planners had a plan for a significant widening of Avenida Atlântica (the avenue next to the beach in Copacabana). If memory serves me there were only two lanes in 1967, one lane each direction. The plan is for two or three lanes in each direction. So where does this space come from? That's where it gets complicated and Rio planners are divising an amazing project: they dig tunnels and bring many hundreds of thousands of tons of sands through them with the effect of broadening or widening the beach itself. And space will be created for the new "multi-lane highway." It is a huge success envisioning a large, wide avenue with many lanes of traffic. There is only one problem: together with this engineering feat come others - the massive increase in the production of steel, the subsequent mass production of automobiles, the creation of easy-credit plans for folks to buy cars, and the seemingly exponential increase in traffic on the roads of Brazil's large cities, particularly São Paulo, but with Rio de Janeiro, Belo Horizonte, Salvador and Recife not far behind. So, there are still massive traffic jams in Copacabana. In 1969 there were only two ways to get from the south zone (Leblon, Ipanema, Copacabana) to downtown: one through the center of Copacabana via Avenida Nossa Senhora da Copacabana or Avenida Atlântica to the east, through the tunnel to Botafogo, and over the viaducts to the "Aterro" in Botafogo, or "the back way," through Ipanema and Leblon, around the Rodrigo de Freitas Lake, through the tunnel to the back of Botafogo, down jammed main streets of Botafogo, back to the main street on the beach at Botafogo Bay and on to the "Aterro" of Botafogo to downtown. Normal life and traffic were characterized by terrible traffic jams no matter which route one chose.

In the back part of Botafogo there is a huge "favela" on top of the hills. They say there is a government plan to bulldoze the "favela" and move all the people out to a "proletarian housing district" in the "Baixada Fluminense." There have been some "mysterious" fires in the "favelas," thus accomplishing the task. Another case is the "Praia do Pinto" Favela behind Leblon. It was announced that it soon would be leveled in the name of "progress." When the inhabitants refused, there was a "mysterious" fire and it was destroyed. Similar events took place in the "invasões" in Salvador or the "mangues" or "mucambos" of Recife. It makes sense that the "povão" does not want to move from the "favelas" in the center of Rio to the "Proletarian" districts in the Baixada, a region known for its terrible pollution, climate, disease and crime. These people work in Rio as door men, maids, washing ladies, construction workers and the like, and the increased cost of train or bus fare into Rio is just one of the good reasons to not want to move. But "progress" leveled the "Praia do Pinto" and the next step is due to be Rio's largest "favela" on the other side of the "Lagoa."

Research in Rio could not wait long; I had a plan to revisit the Northeastern Fair in São Cristóvão in Rio's north zone. Early in the morning, on a Sunday, I caught the bus in the South Zone; it was loaded with maids, doormen, construction workers, many from the Northeast, taking advantage of their day off to "kill homesickness" ["matar saudades"] at the market. It was a cloudy morning but arriving to the downtown and to the north zone there was considerable pollution caused by the traffic, the buses and the factories in the north zone of Rio. Before that however one saw the beautiful Botafogo Bay (polluted itself) in the distance, the clouds up above, Sugar Loaf in the distance, the beaches now replete with people playing soccer in the league and make-up games, but few daring to go in to the water at Botafogo due to that nasty polluted water.

The bus was from the line "Jacaré-Jardim de Aláh" ["Alligator- Allah's Garden"] and I think there may be something symbolic in all that. Jardim de Alah is a beautiful park in the south beach district of Leblon and Jacaré is a poor suburb in Rio's North Zone. The bus was jam packed by the time we got out of Ipanema, the majority of the passengers of dark complexion and short, the stereotypical Northeasterners.

Now in downtown Rio, the center of town, after leaving Avenue Getúlio Vargas on the way to the North Zone, and the many tall buildings of Avenida Rio Branco, there was complete deterioration at the side of the streets. One could see the old 19th century three-story buildings, poorly cared for, beat up, old warehouses, some in the process of being bulldozed. To the right there was a hill with a "favela" almost invisible through the fog and the smog, and on the back side of the hills separating the north and south zones, the north side was full of poor construction.

After a bit, heading west on Presidente Vargas the bus curved and entered "Avenida Brasil," which passed by factories, a canal pitch black with evil, badly smelling "water," the color of coal from the factories. Later after passing through the district of Meier, we arrived at São Cristóvão, its plaza being the connecting point of bus, train and cargo trucks from the northeast and north and west of Rio. To the side of the plaza was São Cristóvão Pavilion, the fair or market surrounding it on three sides. The fair is the "home away from home" for the northeasterners ["pau de arara, caipira"] who frequent the scene each Sunday morning. This particular Sunday the fair shares its space with the "National Beer Festival" inside the pavilion, a less than healthy circumstance.

Folklorist Raul Lody has written the best and most detailed description of the fair that I know of, all in a long article for the "Revista da Campanha de Folclore Nacional" of Rio de Janeiro. The stands in the fair sell almost everything one could find in Caruaru or Campina Grande or Feira de Santana in the old Northeast: all types of food, tools, household needs, clothing, and hammocks. Folk culture of the Northeast is readily evident: blind folk singers, "forró" trios – sound box, triangle and drums – the kind of music Luís Gonzaga was making famous throughout Brazil in those days. One needs to recall his song, the "Anthem of the Northeast," "Asa Branca" ["White Wing"]. This author comes close to tears each time he hears it! The trios play "bião, xote" and other northeastern rhythms. There are vendors of popular medicines and remedies, preachers of the Bible with the Good Book in hand, snake charmers, and "sword swallowers' and "fire swallowers" as well.

My special interest was the presence of the "Literatura de Cordel" and its sellers and poets singing or declaiming their verse. The poets of "Cordel" as well as the "singer-poets" are more present than in my last visit of 1967. Principal among them is José João dos Santos (Azulão) living now in the State of Rio de Janeiro, but originally from Paraíba. He sells using a small sound system with a microphone (the strident roar of the "forró" music in the fair creates a tremendous obstacle to the poets). He is well turned out, clean, close shaved, and perhaps gaining a kilo or two from the last time I saw him in 1967. He has a female assistant who works as "money collector" while he "sings" or recites the "Cordel" story. Azulão sings and declaims among the best of the "cordel" tradition, this by virtue of the fact he is both accomplished "cantador" and "poeta de Cordel." The audience is impressive, both in the number of persons surrounding the poet and their enthusiasm. While I was there, he sang "The Man on the Moon" and sold many copies of the same. He was kept quite busy with his audience, so I tried to stay out of the way and not draw any attention (the "gringo" was quite evident in the market). Azulão had story poems in the two styles of the times: the traditional covers of the northeastern story-poems and those by Editorial Prelúdio of São Paulo with the colored covers with a sort of "comic book" cover design. I noted the customers seemed to prefer the São Paulo design.

The "Cordel" poet Antônio Oliveira was also present (I had met him in 1967) with a good stock of poems, among them the "classics" of Ceará and Pernambuco States. He was an old veteran of São Cristóvão. And I spotted three or four other vendors as well.

There was a "dupla" or pair of poet-singers, that is, improvisers of verse, nearby, the two in dark suits, with white shirts and ties. They were seated on wooden boxes under the shade of a tree. When I arrived and indicated I wanted to take a photo, they immediately launched into improvised verse, singing poetically of the "foreign guy" who had just arrived. I offered a tip and the improvisation went on.

All in all, the totality of "Cordel" poets and singer-poets was the best that I had seen in this trip to Brazil. It seemed like the Fair was indeed prospering.

I was still on the "make" for publications; man does not live by beach and music alone. I would make contact with the people at the "National Folklore Campaign" in Rio and would surprisingly find a quality place for my first serious, published academic article in the Campaign's nationally recognized journal. And one thing would lead to another – more contacts with the music scene in Rio and northeastern culture as well. But first things first.

On that limited budget I had to be careful to find a reasonable place to live. I was able to get a spot at that same boarding house as in 1967 in Posto 6 in between Copacabana and Ipanema. The same cranky old widow, Dona Júlia and her nervous daughter, Dona Janaína were still in charge and the price and especially the location was right. Even though I had that Assistant Professor salary back in Lincoln, the summer grant money was indeed modest, so monetarily I wasn't that much better off than in 1967. I could swim at Copacabana or Ipanema, take the city bus downtown to the Folklore Institute or to the Casa de Rui Barbosa in Botafogo, and take a deep breath on Sunday mornings and grab the "Jardim de Alah" bus full of rowdy northeasterners on the way to the fair.

8

CRISTINA MARIA – A ROMANTIC REPRISE

What I have not said, and the reader of "Letters" of 1966-1967 might recall, is that Cristina Maria lived just down and across the street from the boarding apartment, itself in a twelve-story building. I called right away, got her on the phone and was invited to come over, all this the day after moving in at the "pensão." She said over the phone, "Your Portuguese is great! What happened?" (As if it was lousy before!) I said, "Nothing like teaching Brazilian Portuguese grammar and speaking five days a week this past year can hurt! My local speaking is rusty, but it will come back quickly. Hey, we have a lot to catch up on Cristina Maria. Are you anxious to see me again?" There was a bit of hesitation on the line, but then a hint of what was to come, "I think we can take up where we left off and maybe fill in some blanks, okay? I've got a lot of news for you."

She met me at the door the next night, took my hands in hers, and gave me that "carioca" cheek kiss but nudging up to me with that voluptuous body. Nothing was wrong with the plumbing or the chemistry as the bulge in my pants might have revealed to her. She brushed against me in recognition. "Gaherty, I said to myself, you've got to control yourself!"

I was ushered into the living room where most of the family were awaiting, Jaime her Dad, her Mom Regina, her grandmother, and her two rowdy brothers, now teenagers. You can imagine the scene: they were recalling the days of 1967, asking me about all the changes since and congratulating me for the Ph.D., the teaching position and full of curiosity about life in Nebraska and Lincoln. (Brazilians have a knack of finding out a lot more than they need to know with just a few telling questions. i.e.

if you are living alone in an apartment you must not be "attached" yet, if you have a nice car, money must not be a problem, and if you are researching once again, the job must be good. We would have several occasions to talk politics, the changes in both the U.S. and Brazil I've already written about. I was up front with my new status - doing the second volume of "Letters" for the "Times" and the semi-diplomatic status for the reporting to the INR -WHA on news stories from "Cordel." I would find out soon enough Jaime's reaction to all that. He was a little more reticent about things Brazilian but would only open up to me once he was sure once again where my sentiments lay.

After promising to be back again the next night I was ushered to the door by Cristina Maria and we both agreed to go back to the "Castelinho" the next night for a beer or two and to rekindle the friendship.

I almost didn't make it. On the way downtown that morning to do research at the Folklore Institute, I got one of those "unlucky" crazy bus drivers for the trip via the "aterro" or semi-freeway from Botafogo to Flamengo and Gloria and then downtown. After the tunnel between Copacabana and Botafogo, the bus speeded up and my "guy" had a shit -eating grin on his face as he stared out the window to the bus on the left; both gunned their motors and the race was on. But not for long. The Jacaré (north zone) bus on the left soon left us in the "dust," until we heard the screeching brakes and crash up ahead; the lunatic had entered the viaduct too fact and flipped over the edge. Our guy let out a "Merda! Foda!" and slammed on his brakes and we veered through the viaduct and continued on our way. I could hear screams, sirens, police cars and ambulances behind us and coming toward us on the other side of the four-lane freeway.

It was not all that uncommon an event, but most times it was on Sunday morning when the "nordestino" bus jockeys raced when there was very little traffic and they were on their way to the north zone and the São Cristóvão Northeastern Market. As mentioned earlier, I made the trip almost each Sunday morning to catch the fair, talk to the "Cordel" poets and buy new story-poems. There was a new one, apropos to the viaduct tragedy, by a fine poet with a nickname of "Mocó" – "The Life of the Bus Driver and Rear Door Collector in Rio de Janeiro." I reported on it in the "Letter" to Hansen because it told the real story of the nitty-gritty life of the poor northeasterners who keep the buses going, providing minimum safety but a cheap ride to your destination. Tales of long hours, all illegal according to the supposed transportation rules issued by the mayoralty in Rio, the absolute lack of break times, drivers having to gulp down a cheese sandwich and a Guaraná for lunch, and worst of all, having their wages garnered when the damned broken-down buses even have a flat

tire. And this not even to speak of the lack of air conditioning during those sauna –
like Rio summers, constant complaints of the poor customers, and to top it all, the
robberies by petty thieves and gang members. The bus company makes the drivers
reimburse the missing case from fares.

The reading of story-poems in the stuffy, tiny library of the Folklore Institute and
putting up with the Director's non-stop cigarette smoking and lousy air circulation,
was still a relief compared to the scare that morning. On a break for lunch I went to
that new fast food place in Rio – "Rick's" ["comida a viagem"] and experienced one
of the finest, small cultural moments I ever had in Rio – the painting of the National
Library which was just across the street. It was an unforgettable scene. For me it is
the epitome of the Brazilian "jeito" or "quick fix." For thirty minutes I watched the
following:

Two men were painting the National Library. They were on a scaffold hanging from
the third story roof of the building and were painting the exterior wall below. Due to
the architectural plan or design of the building there were many "indented" sections
in the walls. Not being able to reach said wall with their paint brushes they found the
Brazilian "jeito:" they rocked the scaffold in a slow back and forth motion, first into
the "crevice," then out. And in that swinging rhythm of back and forth, "whoosh,
whoosh," they would make a couple of passes with the paint brushes. It seemed to be in
waltz time: Ta ta ta TA DA, paint –paint, paint –paint; Ta Ta ta TA DA, paint – paint,
paint – paint. Even the house painters in Brazil are "dancers" and artists! (It made for a
great note in the next "Letter.")

Just another typical day in Rio you say? That evening was not so typical. After a
slow bus ride home to the boarding house in Copacabana, a shower, shave and getting
myself decent, I walked across the street to Cristina's apartment, did all the courtesies
to her Mom and Dad, the "abraços," chats and told of the episodes of the day. They
all hee-hawed at the Library painters' story but were not surprised by the viaduct
story. They had seen it on the nightly "Repórter Esso" network TV news in all the
gory detail – several passengers and the bus driver killed, all others seriously injured
and taken to the "public" hospital (that most Brazilians count as a doorway to the
cemetery). Jaime said, "It's all too common, just another facet of life in a country where
there are no serious regulations or consequences for something that should not and
could have been avoided." I did wonder what if I had been on that other bus! I don't
think I commented before that the Ferreira family like most upper-class Brazilians
never rode the bus (except for the kids' school buses) but took a taxi or drove the family

car themselves. I'm not sure the taxis were much of an improvement over the buses, maybe.

Cristina had told the family we had a "date" and would just be out a short while, walking the short distance to the Castelinho, a respected and "cool" place for young Cariocas to hang out. We did the goodbyes, the "abraços" and hit the street, maybe taking just ten to fifteen minutes to walk there and find a seat in one of those back booths so familiar from two years earlier.

The place was crowded, mostly young "Cariocas," boisterous with that "pé sujo" ["corner bar"] loud conversation, lots of laughing and most everyone drinking "choppe" or draft beer or a few with the "caipirinhas." You could tell this was a "south zone" upper class bar-restaurant by the clientele (my god, this was Ipanema and a hangout for folks like Chico Buarque de Hollanda, and Tom Jobim and Vinicius de Morais on the nights they were not at the "Garota de Ipanema") – mainly whites with just a few blacks, but all dressed in the acceptable attire of the day – the guys in nice jeans or slacks, leather loafers and no socks, tight dress short-sleeved shirts and maybe some jewelry – rings, nice watches, even a gold "collar." The girls, just the sight of them, made this gringo sit up and soon take notice: in very tight jeans with short high heeled shoes, and a blouse that was skin tight and nicely low cut to reveal gorgeous "carioca" sun-tanned breasts (how many were enhanced by Ivô Pitangy, Brazil's internationally acclaimed plastic surgeon in a big and necessary industry in a country with beaches and oceans the main attraction?). Hair style varied but none of the chicks had missed the weekly salon appointment.

Cristina held her own with this crowd. Now in her early twenties, her well-rounded body I recalled so well from 1967 had filled out even more. She was luscious! The small waist, the nicely turned hips and legs and a very ample, full bust, noticed with a nice jiggle just when we were walking to the bar, but not with the low-cut blouse this time – Mom had been aware and casually inspecting her daughter's attire for being with the American. She was not heavily made up and did not need to be, but fresh lipstick and some light eye shadow and mascara highlighted her natural looks. Cristina Maria was not the white Caucasian type you might expect to see in Lisbon but was very much in line with most Brazilian women – this after all was a country of 500 years of mixture of race, and even the most illustrious families showed evidence of a tryst here and there of the ancestors - white plantation owners with black slaves or even Indians. Her complexion was like Jorge Amado's heroines, but if not "clove and cinnamon" at least "clove and honey."

We ordered the "choppe" and with cashew nuts to munch on and really began our reunion from those torrid times two years earlier. There was a lot of water under the bridge. Both of us had matured, but in quite different ways and in totally different worlds. She wanted to know how the dissertation had come out, all the gory details of the defense, and how in the world I ended up at Nebraska. Her type of Brazilian likes Harvard, Yale, Berkeley or Stanford and if they ski, they go to Aspen. But they respect the Jesuits and in fact put them on a pedestal, so the degree from Georgetown was fine. And of course she noted I was not married yet, but had the bachelor life of a young professor doing well albeit in Nebraska.

I think it took a couple of rounds to explain how I damned near did not finish the dissertation due to a disagreement with a pedantic director who did not seem to ever understand that the "Cordel" was folk-popular poetry and not erudite, lyric poetry. He wanted a sophisticated critical treatise; I wanted an informative account, journalistic and historic in nature, on narrative poetry that told of Brazil and the Brazilians. The Jesuit head of the department when he learned of this damn nearly kicked me out of the program. The Jesuit took over the dissertation advising and somehow got me through the four short chapters by June 1968. I told Cristina I chose Nebraska to be closer to family, and she (and all Brazilians) had no problem understanding that. And I filled her in, most importantly, on the success of the first volume of "Letters" for the New York Times in 1966-1967 and my new arrangement: continued research on the "Cordel" and Brazilian Literature, but with new "Letters" to the Times and also the semi-diplomatic visa from the INR. She balked at this, coming from family connections and anti-US government views, but when I explained that it all boiled down to just reporting on events and times in Brazil, especially any story-poems reflecting the goings-on in Brazil, she was okay with that. I told her of the great success in Brazil with Ariano Suassuna and the first book soon to come out. Her people and most highly educated Brazilians held such scholarship and publication in high esteem.

She filled me in on the last two years in her life, one item being startling and a bit of a shock: like the kids of most upper-class Brazilian families, she had earned ("wangled") a one-year study grant to the U.S. to learn English, but they had assigned her to Bessemer, Alabama and to an incredibly racist family. She put up with it, bit her tongue, learned some English, was introduced to the deep, old South, but told me that night in the Castelinho, "I'm never going back to your country. What I saw and experienced was despicable. They can all go to hell." She returned home, did the incredible study for the national college entrance exam and was now enrolled at the

Federal University in Rio in economics and political science. This was the accustomed first step to Law.

Maybe the reader can appreciate my shock – after all yet unexplained to Cristina Maria – one of the purposes of this trip for me was to see if we still "clicked," if there was a mutual attraction that might lead to a more serious relationship and who knows what.

One thing had not changed – the physical attraction and the hormones. Holding her hand, I dared to kiss her on the lips in a modest return to us. It turned out to be a lot more physical than that – tongues intermeshing, lips joined and a need to take a breath. She looked into my eyes, I into hers, and we both knew that we had missed each other. So it all evolved, my hands clutching and rubbing her breasts through the light, thin material of her blouse, her nipples hardening to the touch. When I put a hand on her thigh, she moved it to that warm, soft sex. Whoa Gaherty!

Things were moving a little fast. I ordered more beer and we probably sat and necked for another thirty minutes, oblivious to the others and to the MPB music playing in the bar. Suddenly she said, "We've got to get going." After a visit to the ladies' room to repair her makeup, we exited the bar and returned "home" with a walk along the sidewalk of Ipanema. At the door, I said I'll see you soon and gave her a light kiss. She returned it, said "There's a lot to discuss but I think we can enjoy your time here this summer and maybe, just maybe, I can help out the research along with some fun times. My parents like you – you are a young, Catholic, professional young man they respect. At least enough to let me hang out with you. Mike, I like you very, very much."

Did my feet touch the ground on the way home? I dunno. I was jolted out of my daydreaming by the next few minutes. I don't want to make a big deal out of it, but it was "déjà vu all over again." You might have guessed it – there was a visitor and encounter on the doorstep of my apartment building as I walked the few blocks home. Heitor Dias of the Rio DOPS was leaning against the fender of a black sedan parked near the boarding house building. Like Geroaldo in Recife he gave me a half-hearted "abraço" and said, "Oi Miguel! We're all glad you are back in Brazil and working for the right side this time! You've put on some weight, must be the three steadies with the new job! Ha ha ha. The INR connection with Iverson, your semi-diplomatic visa and connection to the NYT certainly puts you in good stead with us. How does it feel to be "real people" ['gente'] for a change and not some snotty nosed graduate student? If I've got it right, you are continuing research on the 'Cordel.' I sure as hell don't understand why; for me it's some kind of folk malarkey from the northeastern hillbillies invading our nice city. I understand you are supposed to let INR know if there are any poems shedding light on what's happening here in Brazil. I doubt that very much, but so be it. What I'm more interested in is you taking up again with that sexy Cristina Maria, you don't mind me saying I'd take a piece of that myself? But you ought to know that Jaime Ferreira and his leftist 'cassado' friends are still on our list. I guess we can just leave it at this: if you learn anything at all, hear anything at all that might interest the government, let us know. To the contrary, all kinds of shit may hit the fan. We'll be in touch."

I dared to poke his shoulder and said, "Before you go Heitor, just let me say you'll get no problems from me about the politics, but I really resent that cavalier attitude with Cristina. It's an insult to her and me. I think an apology is in order."

Heitor smiled, snubbed out his cigarette on the sidewalk and said, "Gaherty, all that education and you still haven't gotten your head out of your asshole. You are a guest in our country, albeit with a nice passport and visa, and don't forget it. When you're here a little longer you'll see that we Brazilians talk the same way about all women (except mothers and wives) and guys on the make. That's what makes Rio go around and round – 'the marvelous city' right? No offence intended. I meant it as a 'copliment' or should I say, 'compliment.' If you've got a shit eating grin on your face next time I ask you about her, I'll know how things are going. Okay?"

He climbed into the car, waved for the driver to go forward, and I was left pondering life in 1969 in Rio.

9

THE SURPRISE

Life went on, reading "folhetos" at the Casa de Rui Barbosa and National Folklore Institute, the Sunday morning terrifying bus rides to the Fair at São Cristovão and trips to Ipanema beach with Cristina Maria when we could swing it (under Mom's approving eye and "okay," but with little sister Olívia tagging along as chaperone!) Nossa Senhora! Who could believe it? Still?

Cristina had evolved from that two -piece but yet modest not quite bikini of 1967 (still with plenty of tanned skin and a suggestive view of her nice breasts) to the current "rage" for aspiring young "Cariocas" in the South Zone – a full-fledged Brazilian bikini. It was small on the bottom but covered her nice buns and front adequately. But the revelation from the Castelhinho a few nights earlier was indeed certified and revealed by a low cut bikini top. It was all I could do to not have an erection right there when she first peeled off the mandatory top "dress-covering" for the women going to the beach in Rio. Okay, the truth, I did, but lay on my stomach making small talk, thinking of other things until it subsided. Time was spent roasting in the Rio sun, quick trips to the beach and the jump into the icy waves, doing some body surfing, swimming and drying off in the sun. Lots of chit-chat and small talk marked those times. Cristina did say that on the next week the family wanted me over for a nice Sunday dinner and a serious conversation about Brazil. Query: are they checking me out for some kind of future deal?

Then came the surprise – not for "Letters" to the "Times." It was later in that off and on "hot" Rio "winter" on one of our outings to the "Castelinho" that Cristina holding my hand to hers in that back booth, said, "Miguel, I think it's time you did something really Brazilian and really "Carioca." What do you think?"

"If you mean going to the Maracaná for a 'futebol' game, I'm not so interested. I've been to the museums, to the beaches, to Sugar Loaf and Corcovado, boat ride in the Bay, so what's up?"

"Mike, do you know about our Motels? I think it is time you had that experience. If you can come up with $100 in 'expenses,' I can handle the rest."

"Cristina, do you mean what I think you mean? 'Nossa,' I presume you mean going with you? If this is what I think it is, we are taking an exponential step from the Castelinho."

She nudged me, smiled in a way I had not seen before and said, "I think we're ready. Didn't I promise you some fun this winter? I'll tell my folks I'm going to Parati with some girlfriends and their families (we do it all the time), leaving on a Saturday morning and back late Sunday. Cariocas do that weekend often. I've got a friend with a new "Fusca" she will be glad to loan me, I'll pick you up in front of the Othon in Copacabana early Saturday afternoon and we'll make a day and night of it. And a friend of hers owns the Motel which makes it even better. It's a kind of a 'gift' to me; she knows about you and approves of our moving things a little farther down the line! And I guess you ought to have surmised by now, this is just an advanced 'Carioca' version of what those people in Alabama called 'a hot date.' The car's taken care of, the 'tariff' for the 'Motel' too; you just have to pay for incidentals. Oh, and by the way, you don't have to spend a wad on condoms, I've taken care of all that. Just don't 'shoot your wad' too soon."

I was in a bit of shock hearing all this from my sweet but evidently not so innocent Cristina, but I guess the taxi driver from another trip was right when he said all the women in Rio like to screw, some just like to screw more than others. But I think this was a little bit different or at least I hoped so, after all, I had not mentioned so far any "designs" on our future. I said, "Topo." ["I'm all in."] But I have to know, is this just another 'Aventura' for the sex for you?"

Cristina said, "Bobo, ['dummy'] what do you think? I admit I did this one time before with a guy I was sure was 'the one' and it turned out to be a disaster. The 'puto' was queer as a three- 'cruzeiro' bill! I have no doubts about you in that regard, not two years ago and certainly not now. But 'querido' you mean a lot to me and I want to be sure we are, as they say, 'compatible' in every way. I don't deny the fun though, intimacy and the bedroom heat! But you are buying the champagne and 'tira-gostos' and paying the tip. Are you up to this? If you are, I'll pick you up next Saturday, 4 p.m. in front of the hotel; I'll be in a blue, new 'Fusca.' You might bring a small travel bag, but that's no news in front of a hotel."

"Saturday already? Okay, hey, let's do it. I'll tell my nosy boarding house 'mom' I'm off to Petropolis for the weekend. She suspects I'm on the make anyway and will be glad to see me 'relax' a bit." And I've been on a couple of all nighters in the bars, so I'll just get the usual 'grilling' when I get back. I'll be the gringo-looking guy on the curb in front of the hotel. Any particular dress code for this place?"

"Are you kidding? We drive the car into a motel 'apartment' garage, private entrance, close the garage door, and take the elevator up to our suite. If it weren't for the drive you could already be 'peludo,' ['naked'] but hey that would take some of the anticipation and surprise out of it? Just dress (and undress) to please me."

Time went by in a hurry and there were some nervous moments. I never dressed "scruffy" in Brazil but did not exactly come up to "carioca" standards. I had nice slacks and shirt, but that white J.C. Penney Nebraska underwear would not cut it. So, I asked a Brazilian buddy where a good shop was to get a "sunga" style underwear short for such an occasion (the same guy who told me over lunch one day, "Gaherty, you must be extremely exhausted." I said, "Why?" He said, "Pois, you are a rich 'gringo,' not at all bad looking, like women, so what else is there to say?") I wish!

Saturday rolled around; the big day had come! I had this tiny duffel under my arm waiting out on the "calçada" in front of the Othon, and right on time at 4:00 p.m. this shiny "Fuscão" [Large VW "Bug"] pulled up, beeped the horn twice and I looked in at a dazzling Cristina in a bright blue sheath dress she had to have been poured in to. "Oi," Pronto"? "Você deveria estar brincando"! ["You must be kidding!"]

Cristina expertly pulled out into the busy Avenida Atlântica traffic and headed west toward the Fort, traversed the four or five blocks through the back of Copacabana and got on the main traffic artery cutting from the canal at Ipanema-Leblon and back around the Lagoa Rodrigo de Freitas and then the long tunnel under Corcovado to the North Zone. I was lost by this time but soon recognized the main avenue in Barra. The whole time she had Chico Buarque on the CD player. "Gosta? É p'ra matar saudades."

We slowed down still along one of the busy commercial streets in front of what seemed a three-story apartment building but with an iron gate and garage door behind it. She beeped the horn, a uniformed attendant appeared, pushed a button alongside and the gate opened up, the garage door behind it and we drove into what was a darkly paneled room with just enough room for the car, an area to either side, and an elevator in front. Cristina grabbed an overnight bag from the back seat, told me to grab my duffel and pushed the elevator button. The door immediately opened, and we were whisked up to the third floor where it opened into a richly decorated, three room "apartment" with a "living," kitchen, bath and an elaborately appointed bedroom.

Cristina threw her bag on the bed, turned around and enveloped me in a tight embrace and kissed me deeply while running one hand through my crew cut gringo hair and with the other feeling my buns. I in turn dropped the duffel and returned the favor. After a moment, a bit "arfando" [out of breath] she said, "Check the dinette and the frig." There was an elaborate lay out of all kinds of "tira-gostos" – boiled shrimp in sauce, salmon, tiny sandwiches, and several kinds of bits of cheese and olives. In the frigo bar were several bottles of champagne, Brahma and Xingu beer and bottles of "tinto" and "branco" wine from Rio Grande do Sul. She said, "You will need all the energy you can get, so let's eat up, open the champagne and then take a shower from the heat from the ride."

The bath was elaborate, the shower obviously meant for two, with gold faucets and shiny white ivory, but then who noticed! We took our time helping each other out of those "car" clothes and Cristina revealed her entire self to me, long shapely tanned legs and waist and lovely chest and arms and shoulders, but her sex surrounded by a tiny band of less tanned bikini skin. Before I could lather her and myself up, she produced this fruit flavored jelly-like substance from a small bottle and rubbed it all over my fully inflamed penis. She laughed, saying, 'You know we Ferreiras are all from Pará originally and the Amazon forest has secrets – this is one of them. It's from the açai berries but mixed with some other forest goodies that will drive you crazy. I think a little Brazilian '69' is in order before the main course. There was a large shelf on the side of the shower where one could lean or half-way sit and we took turns on each other, this after she had spread the "jelly" generously on her vagina. My god it did drive me crazy and when she returned the favor, I lasted just a minute before the "explosion." "I'm sorry, merda, that was over way too quick." She laughed again, saying, don't worry, it just shows you are a red-blooded normal guy who appreciates a bit of TLC from a Brazil connection. And hey, I've got a few surprises to take care of this. The day and night are young, and we can fix up your libido in a hurry." Already rising again to the occasion, I returned the favor, nibbling and then licking my tongue on her clitoris until she shuddered with pleasure, saying, "Mais, mais, outra vez, mete o dedo and esfrega ai!" She came again, and both of us satiated for the moment, did indeed give each other a fragrant rub down and lathering up and toweling down in the shower.

Gathering the champagne glasses, filling them again and putting the "tira-gostos" to the side of the bed, we rested and mainly enjoyed each other's company. Cristina disappeared into the living room, grabbed something from her night bag, ran into the bathroom and in a moment came out in this lacy, white, tight bodiced top which left room for her ample breasts to tease me, and a tiny "fio dental" bottom. Aroused again, we toasted each other, and this time lay on the bed, she puffed it up with pillows and proceed to make passionate love. Her nipples, firm as berries and as delicious (the jelly was rubbed on them), her vagina inviting and her kisses long and hot (and with some fruity taste as well) and my body now scented with the bath fragrance and my penis erect as well, all made for a satisfying, moaning ascent to climax.

Later, sweating and a bit out of breath, back to "rest," we talked and laughed and basically swore that this was great and meant to be. I wanted then to tell her of my deep passion for her and how I hoped we would live our lives together, but she put a finger to my lips, said, "Hush, just enjoy the moment." More champagne, soft music, and then Cristina said, "There's a bell over there. We'll get semi-decent and ring for dinner. I suggest the 'lagosta, bife a milanesa, e petti-pois' with a nice white wine."

"How do you know all about this? Cristina, I know you are not a 'pro,' but only professionals back home could manage this." She said, "I told you I was here once before, we enjoyed it all minus the sex. But give a girl some credit; this comes naturally to a well - raised Brazilian girl! Then she giggled, gave me a long kiss and said, go ahead and push the bell."

After a sumptuous repast, two glasses of fine wine, and a "chique" uniformed maid cleared all, Cristina said, "Let's talk. Down to business before some more pleasure. I want you to tell me exactly what the deal is on your research, your professional and diplomatic status and what you want to accomplish this "winter" and then we can develop a plan."

"Do we have to? Why waste time? All right, as you wish. I opened a fresh bottle of champagne, poured us a glass to share and repeated what I've already written in my introduction to 'Letters II.'

"I'm here for just three months during your 'winter' to accomplish two main things: first, peddle my dissertation in Brazil and begin to get some publications, this is just to keep my job, get tenure and be promoted at Nebraska. And I'm already over the top with success on that – the small book at U. of Pernambuco Press 'sponsored' by no less than Ariano Suassuna. Icing on the cake is my first academic article in the National Folklore Review, already reviewed and accepted by the Campaign for Folklore here in Rio. It's far more than I even expected to accomplish.

"The second main part of the plan is to continue research on the story-poems of 'Cordel;' they are going to be my 'bread and butter' the next few years in academia. And aside from that, I truly believe they are the best 'document' of a huge part of regional and even national culture in Brazil. I've probably added three hundred 'folhetos' to my collection up in Pernambuco and maybe a hundred so far here at the NE fair in Rio. So all looks good on that account; it will take me several months to read them, digest them and write up a sensible account on their meaning and importance.

"The only thing new and I mentioned it at your house the other night is the INR-WHA connection linked to the reporting and 'Letters' for the 'Times.'"

Cristina, no academic "klutz," nodded, seemed to absorb what I had said and then took my hand in hers, looked me in the eyes, and said, "I think I can help you improve on all that; I've had this idea ever since you wrote and told me you were coming. Bear with me and I'll try to give you the short version.

"As I understand it, you want to report on your experiences here like in 'Letters I' – life in Brazil, the people you meet, even the hum-drum of daily life – but hey not me and the motel! And you want to give this bigger picture of life between the lines – how the government, the politics, the regime and its oppression are affecting the 'nordestinos.' I think you should shoot higher, make your reporting larger to reflect not just the 'nordestinos' but all of us in dealing with this dire situation in my country. And the vehicle may come as a surprise to you and combine what you love best about Brazil (except me and hot sex) with quality reporting. Are you ready? Two words: Chico Buarque. You remember that as young as he is, he single - handedly did the music for 'Morte e Vida Severina' and we in fact listened to some of that in 1967."

"Jesus, José e Maria" I blurted out. "I'm not sure how in hell I can do what you suggest, but I will tell you that this last year at Nebraska I in fact taught 'Morte e Vida Severina' in the advanced Brazilian Literature Course using the LP and original sound track. Chico is a frigging genius with words and music and matched Melo Neto's poetry. So, I'm all ears but can't figure out the actual 'how' all of this could take place."

Cristina said, "You do know he and Marieta and the baby are in what you might call 'self-exile' in Italy. If you don't know the story, I'll fill you in later at home. He was basically told to not come home, too dangerous. (He had a big concert tour in Italy this year, a proposed LP and basically it all fell through and he and Marieta are living from hand to mouth in Rome.) And you know Geraldo Vandré has disappeared. Caetano is in London. Jair is singing samba for carnival and Nara Leão basically has retired. Chico knows the score, but the truth is he and Marieta are so homesick and want the grandparents so see the baby. That song 'Samba de Orly' says it all. And the Generals, so far, are saying 'Maybe, maybe, but with conditions.'

You had no way of knowing I've got connections to him through Marieta and school days here at the Santa Ursula Colégio. I think you've got to meet Chico, explain all that research you've done, the 'Letters' and show him the dissertation. He had a huge passion and compassion for Northeastern culture."

I interrupted: "Not like his uncle who had that infamous statement putting down "Cordel" in the "Aureliáo."

Cristina continued, "I can introduce you, and you take it from there. I hear he's due back early next year; let's see how it evolves – you've already got your grant proposal and grant for next year's research!

But, hey, there is just one more surprise for you – a little gift from me, but for me as well. It's something we 'nortistas' from Amazonas and Pará know about. She reached into her overnight bag and pulled out this bottle, about the size of an aspirin bottle and with no label. You put a few drops of this on your tongue, wait just a few minutes and you will see why we call this like our city Rio, 'A Cidade Maravilosa,' ["The Marvelous Magic"]. It's made from six different berries from the Amazon; if you like it, I have a 'friend' who carries a suitcase full of the stuff on the Varig Manaus-Belém 747 flights to his 'associates' here in Rio, my Dad one of them as well as his 'macho' friends. It's 'over the counter' and with a very 'hush-hush' formula. Enough 'bullshit,' here, just a few drops on the tongue while I go 'freshen up.'"

Merda, it was bitter, sour to the taste. But I held my nose, did the drops and put my full trust in Cristina. She was back in a flash, now in the same sexy, body-fitting lace and "fio dental," but now bright red. I don't know if it was the sight of her, the drops, or both but friend penis not only stood up and took notice, but kind of like that bamboo in the zoo in Belém, or a plebe at the academy, stood stiff at attention ready for a sexual salute to this female "general" humbly kneeling down before me and beginning to caress the tool. Reader alert: remember this is not for "Letters."

The Gaherty's even with all the Irish blarney are not ones to exaggerate or certainly stretch the truth, but the next few hours were up to that time unsurpassed joy and pleasure. We both finally fell exhausted about six a.m. and slept for a few hours before waking, putting all our stuff back in the bags, and got ready for the return to reality. I left the $100 bill on the bedside table and took a good look around, trying my best for a mental picture. So, this was the famous Carioca Motel, but far more amazing was the natural, affectionate way Miss Cristina Maria "introduced" me to it. She did mention as we drove out the opened garage door, "I assume this would 'curl' those pages of 'Letters' you send to New York, but remember, 'Em boca fechada náo entram moscas' ['Flies can't get into a closed mouth']. So, this little chapter is off limits to the 'Times' right?"

Dropped off at the Othon, Cristina waved goodbye and said, call in a day or two; it's time to have that serious talk with Dad about Brazil (and not us).

Dona Júlia at the boarding house, sniffed when I unlocked the door, and smiled, knowingly, I think. "We wondered what you were up too. I'll just say you must have good taste. That scent of perfume is from expensive stuff, and you seem to be more relaxed than anytime the past few days. Ah to be young again. But the lilies only bloom for a day, enjoy it while you can."

10

JAIME FERREIRA – THE INSIDE STORY

A couple of days later I called Cristina and was invited over for an "aperitivo" and dinner and conversation with her father Jaime. I dressed in my best "casual," sport shirt, slacks and leather loafers and arrived at 6 p.m. Cristina greeted me at the door with a light "carioca" embrace, air kisses, and a smile, saying "How have you been? We've missed you." On this occasion most of the talk with Jaime actually took place before dinner. I asked how he was doing and he informed me that the 10-year taking away ["cassação"] of political rights was still in effect (it started with him in 1966) meaning he could no longer participate in politics at all (in spite of being a former federal congressman from Pará State), could not vote (he laughed at this, "No real elections going on in Brazil anyway") and the DOPS and the SNI had him under constant vigilance. However, he was allowed to continue with the business interests for the most part, concrete companies in the North, but his customers had changed – no longer Czechoslovakia, Hungary or the Soviet Bloc Countries of Eastern Europe, but Portugal, Spain and a smattering of small countries in South America were okay. I gathered the Ferreiras could still pay their bills.

He then moved on to more serious matters in the country since I had last visited in August, almost all I have touched upon earlier in this narrative, but important to repeat coming from him: "Mike, after you left Brazil in August 1967, things grew exponentially worse. The opposition, such as it was, the "Frente Ampla" was closely watched by the government. General Costa e Silva came in late that year and the government immediately began suppressing the liberals of the Catholic Church and members of the UNE (National Student Union). After a student member was killed in a demonstration in Rio, the government prohibited all further manifestations. We all reacted (that is, those of us who were not prohibited by law) and there was a huge protest in Rio in 1968, the 'Passeata dos 100 Mil" [The One Hundred Thousand Person March]. Negotiations with the government by the opposition failed, and the federal police invaded the campus of the University of Brasília (a forward-thinking institution of the times) and closed it down. São Paulo followed shortly by dissolving the 30th Congress of the UNE and arrested its leaders. In that "shell" congress in Brasília a federal deputy had the nerve to defend the UNE and his rights were taken away ("cassados"). I knew the guy well in my day, good friends, and now in the same sad "club."

"It all culminated just last December 13th, 1968 (everybody knows the date). Costa e Silva and the generals promulgated AI-5 (Institutional Act n. 5). The national congress was permanently dissolved with more "cassações" of its members' political rights and complete press censorship became the rule of the land. Since then it is more important to know what you are not hearing than what's reported in the press and on TV. Students have disappeared, some able to speak out of torture and interrogation by the military in cahoots with the DOPS. Religious leaders from the Left have been threatened by para-military groups in Recife, Bahia and here. The only leader they are apparently afraid of is Cardinal Arns in São Paulo; I would say that only the church today can defend us.

"The only 'happy' note to the 'censura previa' is that we Brazilians are resilient, and mainly we are clever. Jouralists and mainly the MPB people are 'driblando a censura' in what's probably the most ingenious intellectual production in Brazil's history."

I interjected at this, "Yes, Cristina Maria has brought me up to date on Chico Buarque, Milton Nascimento, Geraldo Vandré and some of the others. She in fact thinks I should get in contact with Chico when he returns, possibly next year, and see if we can work together on 'reporting' what's really going on in Brazil. But the more I hear, I doubt that either he or I will be in a position to do that. And there is one important item in regard to all this to tell you that you may not be aware of. I'm here this time to do research on the 'Cordel,' working on the academic 'publish or perish' rule, but also to peddle my dissertation and even use chapters in academic journals. I already told Cristina, I've had great success – a small book at the University of Pernambuco Press backed by Ariano Suassuna and my first article at the National Campaign of Folklore.

"But there is a third facet to the work. I don't know if you knew back in 1967 that I was under an agreement with the 'New York Times' to write occasional 'Letters' doing broadscale reporting on what was going on in Brazil. It was a big success; the readers of the International Section of the 'Times' ate it up when I wrote of literature, folklore, the folk poets of 'Cordel,' carnival, the beach and even sex, recounting my own escapades in Brazil. In fact, the 'Times' published all the 'Letters' in a book that has done well. So, they want me to do it all again this time and I've already sent in a 'Letter' or two. What you may not know is how last time ended after I left all of you in March of that year. I traveled up the São Francisco river on one of the 'gaiolas' – great material for the 'Times' and incidentally a connection with Audálio Dantas of 'Realidade' and 'Cruzeiro' fame – got an extension from Fulbright to go to your old stomping grounds in Belém to check out the old 'Cordel' press of Guajarina and then on to Manaus and its poets. I ended the year here back to Recife and met old friends and tied up loose ends. Unfortunately I got caught at the wrong place at the wrong time and not by my own will, got caught up in a student protest near the Law School in Recife, was thrown in jail along with the student protesters, got roughed up, but was freed by my connection to the 'Times' and to the 'INR' but was sent home on the next plane to New York."

I repeated what I've already said before, but this time to Jaime Ferreira; he had to know the whole story, not only because of research in Brazil but because his daughter was involved with me! "The difference now is not only do I have the 'Times' connection, but the INR has given me a diplomatic visa to do the reporting in regard to any 'Cordel' stories reflecting the national scene. I assure you I am on your side and am in full opposition to the dictatorship and all it represents, but like any other real journalist I'm walking a tightrope in doing the stories. The INR wants the full story, whatever it is, but SNI and DOPS want only anything favorable to the regime and to good Brazil-United States relations. So far, in regard to 'Cordel' there has been no problem. The poets cannot afford to be taken to task and like all folk poets, know their time and place. But I can tell you the DOPS agents are watching me and we have had a tangle or two, particularly in Recife at the docks where the Alliance for Progress Food Shipments come in. In essence I've been told 'to watch it.' They know of my friendship with Cristina Maria and your family. So what I'm asking is your take on all this and more important your advice. You need to know I really like your daughter, enjoy her company and when we get to that topic, value her insight and help with my research."

"Mike, you don't have a thing to worry about. All of us who are 'cassados' are fully versed in the DOPS and SNI tactics. Pardon me, but not only it is no problem knowing an American Professor with such connections, but it actually might help dispel some suspicions – hell, what could make Costa e Silva and company happier than to know 'ole Ferreira maybe has turned a new leaf and the family is kibitzing with a 'Times' reporter and INR insider! Thanks for being so up front about it; believe me, Cristina's mother and I welcome you here anytime, and it's no mystery to us that Cristina Maria waxes in superlatives when she talks of you. How long are you going to be here anyway?"

"I'm ticketed for August 31st; classes start in Lincoln September 10th and I've got to be ready for all that. There are always a few loose ends to tie up before classes start. But thank you for your kind words; I hope to be seeing a lot of all of you. Cristina and I have already planned an initial strategy meeting next week on the possible approach and tie-in to Chico Buarque, so you will be seeing a lot of me in those days. And besides, I really want to take her up to the 'Berro D'Agua' in that old hotel superstructure in the back of the Lagoa. I went with 'gringo' friends a few days ago – it undoubtedly has the coolest 'bossa' music and dancing under the stars if you can catch good weather."

You can imagine the scene on the walk back to the boarding house that night. It's "old hat" by now. Heitor was parked as usual just a bit down from the building entrance, once again leaning against the fender and smoking one of his illegal Marlboros ("moamba" or smuggled goods). He smiled this time, even gave me that half-embrace saying, "Oi Miguel, Vamos falar." He offered me a cigarette; I haven't mentioned that I had the curious ability to smoke in Brazil, toss the pack in the trash out at the Galeão Airport and head home to a smokeless Lincoln. So I took him up on it, inhaled that strong American tobacco, not the nasty cheap Brazilian tobacco (I was hooked on it in Recife in 1966 and 1967 so no big deal.) He said, "You remember our agreement, no funny stuff but just letting us know what ole' Ferreira is up to and what he has to say."

I retorted, "I'm not about to be your stooge, I think you know that, but I can share anything I might share with let's say the 'dona' in the Boarding House. Ferreira just reviewed for me the main national news events since I left in late August of 1967, brought me up to date on the government changes, AI-5, censorship, he and others' comportment so as to not break any of the 'cassações' rules, but mainly we talked of my stay here, my research and reporting, all that shit that you already know, and he even laughed thinking the you guys might approve of his friendship with the American and the fact he and his daughter are getting along so well."

"You got that right, so be it. I'll restrain myself about her, don't want to offend you again. We'll know if there is anything interesting to report or talk about. All's 'bacana' [cool] for now. Don't get sunburned and be careful of the 'red flag' days and 'ressaca' [undertow] down at the beach. See you soon. Oh, by the way, we've read all of this year's 'Letters.' I didn't know Brazil could be so interesting. Good job."

11

ROUTINE IN RIO

I don't know if I've written of it, but it's important to know that in these months of "winter" 1969, "Cordel" reflected at least in some small way, the same scene as national journalism. Alongside the regular press, "Cordel" was practically silenced in its opposition to the military, even though there was no lack of material. The poets in their story-poems, as modest and humble as they are, reflected the same thing as the national press – they were silenced by the "censura prévia" and only the major press was able to react with ingenious veiled criticism cloaked in metaphor, double entendre, and in the case of the papers, entire blank spaces where articles should have been and decontextualized photos and even want ads. In the case of "Cordel," poets were unanimous in saying they were not permitted to do poems with "severe criticism." As a result, in July and August of 1969 I found practically no political "Cordel" poems lambasting the Dictatorship. The same would not be true of MPB and developments even before my time in Brazil in 1969, meaning late 1968. That story becomes part of future "Letters."

In the next few weeks, now mid-July and time flying before the "denouement" of 1969 in Brazil, I began to do serious homework on the MPB and the entire flow of activities, politics, arts and music as pertaining to the national political scene, really having to go back to the beginning of the Revolution in 1964. Since none of this was prohibited and had already been on front page in the Brazilian press, DOPS had no objection, as Heitor would tell me, "As long as you relate it to the culture and to the incredible improvements we the Military have made – in effect saving Brazil from Fidel, Ché and Francisco Julião and cohort Miguel de Arrais and bringing Brazil back to its traditional Catholic roots." It didn't exactly turn out that way, but more important events would "trump" my reporting as soon as August."

At the same time with all this serious talk about me and the DOPS, Brazil, and the dictatorship, research was going on, Cristina Maria and I managed to have some memorable moments. One of them was the night I took her to "Lisboa à Noite" to hear "fado" music. I had been there with Don, the Peace Corps Volunteer, in 1967. At the time it was the only way I could really experience Portuguese music (notwithstanding the experience in the Portuguese boarding house in Bahia in 1966).

More important was our evening at the "Berro D'Água" Restaurant and Night Club in a surreal place in the back of Laranjeiras. I had been to the place with fellow Fulbrighter Steve Baldini. The reader of "Letters" might remember him from "Letters I," a Harvard Graduate on a Fulbright in 1966-1967 to do research on economic development in Brazil and a good friend from Recife days and later travel to Brasília. And incidentally, an "unofficial" but paid agent of the infamous CIA. Steve now in 1969 was a full-time employee of Catholic Caritas and involved in management of the same in Rio. He introduced me to the "Berro" with his friends, the daughters of the Library of Congress Representative at the time in Rio.

This place had to be the most unusual but also the "coolest" nightclub in all Brazil. I never did find out the entire story, but the club is in about a 20-story building near the Lagoa de Rodrigo Freitas. Originally meant to be a hotel or apartments, financing fell through and only the concrete and steel super structure, floors and support columns were built. Someone decided to make lemonade out of this big "lemon" and finished the top floor, adding a new elevator to get there. Up on top is the "Berro D'Água" Restaurant and Night Club. The name of the place comes from a "novella" by Jorge Amado: "A Morte e a Morte de Quincas Berro D'Água" ("The Death of Quincas Wateryell" by one translation). The main character Quincas is a real expert on the diverse types of "cachaça" in Salvador, knowing them well by color, "perfume," and taste. On one occasion he is the victim of a joke by his drinking buddies: they serve him a small glass of the "branquinha" which is really water. Quincas slugs it down, chokes, coughs, and spits out the drink, yelling "ÁAAAAGUA."

I can't talk about the restaurant because we never ate there, but I imagine its prices matched the 20-story height. But the Night Club was terrific, when we went, quiet, comfortable, elegant and with good "bossa" music. The highlight was to go to the outdoor dance floor to the side and in good weather witness and live this scene: the

Christ figure and Corcovado in the mist high to the right, the "Lagoa Rodrigo de Freitas" directly ahead, and the Ipanema-Leblon beach district beyond it. It made for spectacular close slow dancing! A memory however is that one had to be extremely careful at the bottom of the building dodging old construction materials to get to the elevator. Anyway, the warmth of the evening and Cristina's spectacular body were like a caress of the warm sea breezes in Bahia.

12

MPB, CHICO BUARQUE DE HOLLANDA, AND A PLAN

Shortly after that spectacular night, when by the way, I took Cristina home with no extra-curricular stops, we were all shaken by events. On August 3rd General Costa e Silva suffered a massive stroke. The Military immediately set the wheels in motion (I'm sure they had contingency plans) for the "succession:" a Junta would be formed and would rule with an iron fist, but temporarily, until a hard-liner General named Garrastazu Médici (how's that for Basque and Italian heritage in Brazil) from Rio Grande do Sul would be duly "elected" and take office the end of 1969. Of course, no one knew on August 3rd exactly what all this would mean, but José Ferreira had no doubts: Brazil would feel the full force of the oppression of the dictatorship. The new man was known to be yet more sanguine than any of his now "milder" predecessors.

We did not really talk that much about all this; we just expected the worst. There was however some "unfinished business" with me and Cristina Maria before I caught that Varig 707 on August 31st. First was the plan for Chico Buarque and then for us.

After all the political developments and our socializing, later toward the end of August with my return to Nebraska imminent, I arranged a meeting to talk to Cristina Maria and hear for the first time her suggested plan for my research, MPB and meeting Chico Buarque de Hollanda, the latter a wild dream for me. Cristina Maria's idea was to incorporate the voice of popular protest in Brazilian Popular Music (MPB) with the reporting on "Cordel" and life in Brazil in general at the end of 1969. She had done her homework and already had a printed file for me to read. The final idea was to rework these first notes into an application for a research project to someone in the U.S. in late 1969, get a research grant, come back to Rio in 1970 and see what would happen.

13

CHICO BUARQUE DE HOLLANDA AND THE MPB

The following is my take on Chico and what I would send in a "Letter" to the "Times" as a preamble to a serious research proposal for 1970 and grant money to return to Brazil. It's all in my words, not yet in the language of the final proposal.

Chico Buarque de Hollanda perhaps the most popular young singer-composer-musician in all Brazil in 1965 and the early Dictatorship comes into my story for several reasons, first of all, because I had absolutely loved his early music tied to "carnival" and "Bossa Nova" and life in those years of euphoria of a great Brazilian "renaissance" in music and popular culture. Incidentally, it was no less than Cristina Maria who had lit this cultural flame in 1967 in our time in Rio. Now in 1969, he is foremost because he is in a period of voluntary exile in Italy; it is rumored he will return to Brazil in 1970 and face the new reality. His tie to me, Mike Gaherty, and my role in 1969 is accidental, but hopefully 1970 will bring a change in that.

Chico had done an amazing thing as a late teenager – compose the music for João Cabral de Melo's amazing "ode" to Northeastern Reality (and indirectly its tie to "Cordel") "Morte e Vida Severina." How this young city kid, Catholic, upper-class, raised in São Paulo, moving to that dynamic cultural climate of Rio only in very late teens, managed to absorb, feel and "translate" the reality of the play to music is amazing. It is the work of a young genius.

But there is a second tie to the Northeast, its culture and "Cordel," perhaps serendipitous, perhaps just a small chapter in Chico's amazing early song writing as a teenager. Chico's composition of a seemingly minor song of his early career - "Pedro Penseiro" ["Peter the Thinker"] caught my attention and would ironically, I think on

Chico's part as well, tie him to one of the major themes of all "Cordel" and incidentally to what has been called the "Northeastern Anthem" in a Russian film documentary on Brazil. This is why I have to meet Chico Buarque, share our common interests and fate in Brazil.

Before getting to them, and to see where all this is heading, I've got to bring the reader of "Letters" the background to my goal of incorporating the voice of popular protest in Brazilian Popualr Music (MPB) with the reporting on "Cordel" and life in Brazil in general at the end of 1969 and 1970. It all started and hopefully will end for me with Chico Buarque.

Chico's Story – Significant Moments

"Tem Mais Samba." 1964. Starting point of Chico's song portfolio.
"Marcha para um Dia de Sol." 1964. Next after "Tem Mais Samba."

Sérgio Buarque de Hollanda, a well-known national historian, is Chico's father. He wrote the famous "Raízes do Brasil" ["Roots of Brazil"]. Sérgio died in 1982. The famous poet, song writer, and non-traditional diplomat Vinicius de Morais was a regular visitor to the Hollanda house in São Paulo during Chico's younger years.

Late 1950s: Chico became obsessed with the national sport of "futebol," and one day would start his own amateur team in a small stadium in the Barra in Rio. His team was called "Politheama."

In 1958 Chico and school buddies came under the influence of the "Ultramontanos" an extreme right religious "cult." To the point of fanaticism. Their parents pulled them out of the organization.

Chico and friends were active in social work; one activity was to distribute blankets to the homeless living under the viaducts in São Paulo.

In 1959 Chico was enamoured with U.S. music, "rock n' roll," but at this time the Brazilian Bossa Nova hit "Chega de Saudade" by João Gilberto stormed Brazil and became Chico's link back to Brazilian music. His sister Miúcha would marry João Gilberto in 1962. It was about this time that Chico would learn bossa nova rhythm; he satirized "iê – iê - iê" Brazilian Rock with friend Touquinho.

1961. As a prank Chico and high school buddies "lifted" a car in São Paulo. All were upper class kids. They were caught, arrested, taken to the station, finger-printed and spent the night in jail before family friends succeeded in getting their release.

Chico appeared on TV shows in 1965, "O Fim da Bossa."

In early 1965, theater director Roberto Freire asked Chico to put to music João Cabral de Melo Neto's famous "Christmas Play" ["Auto de Natal"] "Morte e Vida Severina" for "O Teatro da Universidade Católica" (TUCA) in São Paulo. It was in Freire's house in early 1965 that Chico got up his nerve and sang his samba "Pedro Pedreiro." He finished work on MVS in the middle of 1965. The play had great success in France at the Festival in Nancy in the middle of 1966.

Meanwhile, toward the end of 1965, Chico did his first recordings of "Meu refrão," Olé olá" and the recording headed by "Pedro Pedreiro." (Chico met Tom Jobim the end of 1966 and played "Pedro Pedreiro" for him.) So the real personages of Brazilian music were beginning to get to know this young singer's talent.

Chico's samba "Sonho de um Carnaval" was sung by Geraldo Vandré in the First "Festival da Música Brasileira," TV Excelsior in April 1965.

Amidst all this musical success, back in 1965 the military had prohibited political parties, ended direct elections for president and began to mess with students and especially the universities. Alceu Amoroso Lima the most famous Catholic intellectual in Brazil, called the government actions "cultural terrorism." The anti-military satire "Febeapá" came out and the "Revista Civilização Brasileira" expressing ideas of the Left was at its peak.

Now late 1965, Chico was married to Marieta Severo and living in Rio. He was good friends with Touqinho dating from São Paulo days and met Caetano Veloso of Tropicália fame in 1965. "Farra e serenatas" ["Partying and Song Fests"] in São Paulo.

A significant moment in his career was in October 1966 with the recording of "A Banda" and he sang it in the Second Festival in 1966. Chico had moved to Rio, July 1966 and had done a show called "Meu Refrão" just with his songs in a bar in Rio that winter. In the show he had his first problem with the "censura" with "Tamanduá."

The reader of "Letters" might note that at this time censorship was "suave," and these years of the mid-1960s marked an intense period of culture in Brazil. Glauber Rocha in the cinema, MPB music, "Vidas Secas" in the new wave cinema, Garrincha in "futebol."

In October 1966, as mentioned, the "Festival II" of MPB was on national television via TV Record; Chico won with "A Banda," refused first place and wanted the title divided, so they declared a "tie" with "Disparada" by Geraldo Vandré. It was Chico's first big money, $6800 USD for him and also Geraldo. Chico was renting a one-bedroom apt. on Prado Junior in Copacabana at the time. He began to live the life of an artist-musician with shows all over Brazil, all sold out. There were shows in Portugal, and the "Mug" doll, a result of a night of "farra" ["partying"]. There was no artist's wardrobe, no fancy cars, but chaotic success.

The music festivals, now a national tv extravaganza, continued. In the "III Festival da Musica," in 1967 Edu Lobo and "Ponteio" won; Chico was third with "Roda Viva" Caetano 4th, Gilberto Gil 2nd.

A bit later came the explosion of the "Tropicália" movement which caused the Chico-Caetano Veloso friendship to go by the way. Tropicália wanted something "feio" ["ugly"] and Chico always "bonito." Chico was accused of being "passadista," ["antiquated," old time] by Tropicália fans but responded with his famous phrase of the period, "Nem toda loucura é genial; nem toda lucidez é velha" ["Not all insanity is ingenious; not all lucidity is old"].

By 1968 Brazil was wrapped in an explosive political situation; you were either "for or against" the regime. In the 4th MPB festival, Chico placed second with "Bom Tempo" ["Good Time"] but was very disliked because popular political sentiment was the opposite saying it was bad times with the military. He was being judged as "not being with it." Later his song "Sabiá" was judged the same, mistakenly not seen yet as a modern, second "Canção de Exílio" ["Song of Exile," Brazil's most famous song of anti-slavery by a Bahian poet in the 19th century]. Chico was seen as not really taking part in the criticism of the regime (unlike Geraldo Vandré in the Festival with "Pra não dizer que não falei das flores").

Anyway, the press "decided" Chico was an enemy of Caetano Veloso and his group "Tropicália." This was in spite of the fact that all had participated in a movement against the electric guitar and Brazil's rock - "iê-iê -iê." 1968 saw the straw that broke the camel's back for Chico, no longer considered the "nation's unanimous singer" ["unanidade nacional"].

Things grew worse for Chico. The CCC – "Comando de Caça dos Comunistas" ["Command for the Hunt for Communists"] broke into Chico's show "Roda Viva" in Porto Alegre and closed it down. It turned out not to be Chico's fault; the military criticism was added by the director to the play later, unknown to Chico. The director had totally changed the show, all this in July 1968.

The momentos and lugubrious day of December 13, 1968 arrived. Chico saw the announcement of A I – 5 on television. Now, way back when, Chico had thought the students would organize and prevent a "golpe" [coup] in 1964 and was thinking of preparing Molotov cocktails. He was disillusioned ["decepcionado"] when they did nothing. By 1968 he wanted nothing to do with politics and felt disbelief in the whole thing. He did go to a PCB [Communist Party of Brazil] meeting but never joined, but others associated him with it.

Chico did get involved with CEBRADE ["Centro Brasileiro para a Democracia"] due to the participation of his father Sérgio a famous historian in Brazil. Also involved were the famous architect of Brasília Oscar Neimeyer and others; it was not a communist party, but definitely leftist.

Chico participated in the "Passeata dos Cem Mil" ["The Protest of the 100,000"] not because of being so in favor but for being called a "reactionary" if he did not. Five days later, there were rumors that AI - 5 was out to get him, "You are on a list." Taken at 7 a.m. to the Ministry of the Army on Presidente Vargas to "depor" [testify], they did not like, among other things, "RodaViva" with a scene (that did not happen) of an actor defecating into a military helmet. They let him go that p.m, after threats, but saying he had to have permission to leave the city.

He had at the time a professional "compromisso" [contract] at a festival in France in January of 1969, so he cleared the permission and he and a pregnant Marieta left for it. Chico spent most of that year in Italy with promises of records, shows, success, but they all fell through by December 1969.

Related to this period was former bad news from Brazil: on Dec. 27, 1968; Gilberto Gil and Caetano Veloso had been taken prisoner, heads shaved, later exiled to London in 1969. Now in Italy in 1969 Chico was warned not to go back to Brazil. Vinicius de Morais came to Italy, convinced them to stay and the baby was born in Italy in March 1969. Things got worse, payments on apartment on Rodrigo de Freitas in Rio were overdue, 40 shows were cancelled in Italy; Chico convinced friend Touquinho to come to Italy. There was some work, ending up not paid, jobs set up by what turned out to be crooks. But a "gira" [tour] of 6 weeks with famous black singer Josephine Baker turned up and they made some money to get by. A new contract with Phillips in Brazil came in late 1969 for Chico, $21000 US up front which kept "milk for the babies."

In 1969 still in Italy with best friend Touquino, Chico saw the landing on the moon, read of the first kidnapping of an Ambassador to be exchanged for freedom of leftist political prisoners, the leftist Fernando Gabeira the leader in the kidnapping of the U.S. Ambassador. The Left in Brazil was split into many small, independent groups.

All the above would be "homework" for me back in Nebraska in the Fall, Winter and Spring of late 1969 and early 1970. The priority would be putting together another grant application, this time connecting "Cordel" with the MPB, submitting it to the NEH and the American Philosophical Society in Philadelphia and see if I would have any luck.

14

CRISTINA THE PATRIOT – GAHERTY THE PATRIOT

That same night after the "work" session we were able to walk back to our "ponto" [hangout] the Castelhino for "choppe" and discussion about the future – our future. The same quiet music, the "choppe" and all turned out well, but not what I expected. To cut to the quick, I asked Cristina Maria if we had any real future, if she cared enough about me to think of a more serious arrangement, marriage and a life together.

She quietly took my questions in, paused for a while and said, "If you mean getting married and me going back to the U.S. with you, no, that is not a possibility. I've already told you I want nothing to do with your racist country. On the other hand, if you were to immigrate to Brazil and make a life here for the two of us, that is another matter. Mike, you know Brazil better than any 'gringo,' so you know how important family is, that family sticks together. Merda! We don't even move away from our family's city when we graduate and get jobs and get married. I'm not saying any more and in fact I have not heard what I would call a marriage proposal, but I appreciate we have to take baby steps before things evolve. What do you think?"

It was my turn to pause, this was no laughing matter, Holy Mama, we are talking about our future. I said, "Cristina, I feel very deeply about you, and although an Irish-American Gaherty would have a hard time saying it, I think I love you. I did not know when I left the U.S. in June that you had had that terrible experience in Alabama and that it has colored (pardon the reference) your attitude about my country. I guess I had day dreamed simply of a life as a college prof, at least in the beginning at Nebraska, and this cool, sophisticated Brazilian lady at my side. That idea is dashed is it not? Honestly, as much as I love your country, your culture, your language and am good at it, I'm still a product of my youth - Jesus, I'm a U.S. red-blooded farm boy, a patriot and am greatly relieved when I get on that return flight and say, 'I'm going home.' I think it will always be that way. I don't know what the shit I would do in Brazil, how I would make a living. The Academy in Brazil does not need a FOREIGNER or an AMERICAN to tell them about their own country, and I sure as hell can't teach basic Portuguese here! I've got that undergraduate Business Management degree, but hell, it's all theory, and no practice. You know I turned down a job to do business in Guatemala and Central America back in 1963 for all these same reasons. I would have starved to death."

"Mike, I think you have read between the lines and realized our family situation. Dad and Mom are not hurting financially and in fact are in the top profile of economics in Brazil. The concrete and construction businesses are booming especially now that 'No one can secure this country!' Ha! Dad could and would find a place for you in the business; there are export-import opportunities and at times he needs to deal with American companies. You would be perfect. Could you handle all this?"

"I can't tell you right now, but I can't imagine myself in that cutthroat business world. Languages, literature, culture, folklore, teaching, music, that's all my 'cup of tea.' I have an idea: let me go home and ponder the possibility of living in Brazil with you and your family. In the meantime, I'll go ahead with the 'Cordel' and Chico Buarque plan for next year. We can meet again next June and see how we feel. I know I will miss the good times with you."

"All right. That is a possibility. Of course, the fly in the ointment is what Chico says, and more importantly, what he can do in view of the government censorship keeping such a close eye on him. I don't know if he will want to think of being a 'parceiro' [partner] in your research; I do know he will be interested in it and will help with 'dicas,' [hints] but beyond that who knows."

We left it at that. The plan was to communicate during Nebraska's school year, let Cristina know if my grant application for summer, 1970, was successful, and see how things were shaping up in Brazil.

15

A LAST CONVERSATION – HEITOR DIAS AND THE DOPS

Meanwhile I had a lot on my plate, saying goodbye to my hosts at the Folklore Institute (and checking on the progress of the research article), at the Rui Barbosa Foundation, especially mentor Sebasitão Nunes Batista, one of the sons of Francisco das Chagas Batista, colleague of the great "Cordel" poet Leandro Gomes de Barros in Paraíba in the early 20th century, who had sat across from me at the reading table in the "Cordel" library. And there was packing for the trip. The week passed quickly and before I knew it, I was back at the Galeão waiting to check in on the Varig jet in route to New York at James Hansen's invitation to "wrap up" "Letters" for 1969. A surprise but yet not a surprise was to see Heitor Dias casually strolling toward me in the ticketing area.

He was all smiles and said, "Miguel, você mesmo é um arretado!" [Paraphrased, "Mike you are super 'simpático'!"]. A bit taken aback at the compliment, I retorted, "That's a surprise! Why?" Heitor smiled broadly, saying, "For one thing you kept your gringo ass out of trouble; we didn't have to rough you up or squeeze information out of you. Your research efforts were on the level and the 'Letters' were pretty cool. Congratulations by the way on the coming book and article. I did notice you didn't include that tryst with you know who in the motel in the Barra. That would have made for interesting reading. We were following your car out and back. Don't get your shorts in a bunch, it was just 'business' as far as we are concerned. It's her Dad we are worried about, but you were on the up and up with me about any talks with him. You didn't have much 'Cordel' reporting for us, just that story of the bus drivers in Rio, pretty informative and eye opening I suppose. But, hey, somebody's got to drive the damned buses for us and if they are stupid enough to get flipped over a viaduct, there's a few hundred more begging for the same job. Anyway, it was a pleasure having you. My boss at the SNI says he kind of likes you, first time he has known of a U.S. farmboy – hillbilly from Nebraska. And we are getting to be pretty good friends, maybe next time you can join me and my buddies at that 'pé sujo' [sticky floored bar] on Prado Júnior in Copacabana for some beers and talk. I guarantee you we have funny jokes, and you might be surprised the folks we have stories about, just part of the job. So, have a good trip and keep your nose clean and maybe we'll meet again."

My last words to Heitor were intentionally in that "joking" mood he liked to hear, "Well, Officer Dias, that is all good news. If the DOPS is paying, I'll keep our glasses full and we'll see who can stay upright by 3 in the morning. And maybe you can line me up with some of that 'stray' stuff you guys keep a watch on Saturday nights in Copacabana and Leblon."

16

CHECKING IN WITH JAMES HANSEN

The eight-hour flight to New York went fast enough, I was busy with more notes for the last segment of "Letters" and writing up an initial report to the research committee at the University of Nebraska. James Hansen did not meet me at the airport this time but had a "Times" intern meet me at the gate and take me by taxi to Manhattan from JFK. This time he booked me at the tourist hotel across from Madison Square Garden (along with the mobs of U.S. and foreign travelers), but we had lunch again at that great same great deli near the Garden. Hot pastrami, cheesecake and a couple of icy beers made me feel "back home again." The conversation this time was not charged with any major happenings like my misfortunes in 1967 (narrowly escaping really getting hurt or even killed by the Pernambuco police or that pesky "clap" business). It more like a "debriefing" from the boss.

Still smoking that briar wood pipe, wearing the tweed jacket with patches on the elbows, and a New York reporter's hat, James initiated our post-luncheon talk saying, "Mike, another successful year for your 'Letters!' Albeit, not as lengthy and suspenseful as 1967, but then you were only three months in Brazil and things were not as new. Still, the 'chronicle' hit the main points and had some lively moments for the readers. I don't think it merits another book, at least not quite yet, but we can keep 1969 on file for future 'Letters.' I guess you realize we've got a good thing going, so the NYT and INR-WHA (I'm always in touch with Stanley Iverson) want it to continue. Too much hangs in the balance for Brazil, an important part of the international page coverage here at the 'Times;' we can't afford to ignore it. We are apprehensive about the trend of the dictatorship and certainly what may happen now that General Costa e Silva is out of the mix. I can certainly put in a good word for any grant applications for next year (modestly, that practically guarantees your success), and we of course will keep the same monetary agreement as well as the INR visa in place. Funny, I've got this idea you were leaving something out in your relationship with Cristina Maria, just a hunch you know. Anything to it? Remember we are interested in ALL you do and experience. You kept out of trouble, at least other than that scrape in Recife, and you kept your nose clean with the DOPS. I personally am finding it interesting the evolution of your 'friendship' with Geroaldo and Heitor. They are people who inadvertently or not can add another perspective to your story. So, let's keep in touch about next year. And, oh, what about Molly in D.C.? Seems to me you have a bit of a dilemma on your hands. Trust the Irish! And the Irish Americans! Great writers, musicians, lovers but lousy at keeping it all straight!"

After a long sip of that good Scottish Ale, not a Guinness mind you, I thought a while and said, "Thanks Mr. Hansen, I appreciate your confidence in me and my writing, and I certainly would not mind being affiliated with the 'Times' for years to come if you would have me. As for Cristina Maria, she did show me 'the ropes' of how to have fun in Rio, and I'm not really sure where all that is headed, but definitely there is a 'to be continued' for next year. At the minimum we'll be conferring about research with Chico Buarque, what else, I do not know. And yeah, I've got a date with destiny, a lousy turn of phrase, but true, with Molly after I leave you and New York. Women! What do the British say, 'A sticky wicket' or something like that, I'm not even sure if that's right. Back home in Lincoln we put it a little differently, maybe 'Stuck between a rock and a hard place.' Oh yeah, my Irish-American mom would have put it best: 'That's a fine kittle of fish'."

James paid the tab, we shook hands, and he said, "You always enliven my day. Good luck Mike and we'll be in touch."

17

＊＊＊

MATTERS IN D.C.

I would catch the train down to D.C. the next morning, but a bit of New York happened that evening. I had gotten back to the hotel early, so was a bit hungry and there was this Irish Bar-Restaurant a couple of blocks away. I thought I might hear some good Irish music while drinking a Harp or two, but it turned out to be another lesson for the innocent, but not so innocent farm boy from 1967. The bar was Irish all right with a loud, boisterous crowd of regulars at one end by the door, all talking very loudly, razzing each other over the ball scores that day. I think they were mainly construction workers in the vicinity. But no Irish music was to be had; it was basically an Irish sports bar, so TV screens had all kinds of games going.

I got the Harp, this while sitting up at the bar and had quaffed two or three when this good-looking young chick moved over, a bar stool or two away, introduced herself and the farm boy still isn't sure what the hell all this was about. What commenced was one of the spiciest conversations I had ever had with a chick, all manner of swear words including the "f" word as a noun, verb, adjective, and mainly expletive! (From graduate school days in Spanish, the great Mexican writer Carlos Fuentes did the same thing with a page and a half on "chingar" in one of his novels.) She wondered where I was staying and when I said at that huge but run-down hotel across from the Garden, she laughed, "Oh, that rat hole. I bet the rooms are the size of postage stamps. And you run into the whores in the hallways!" Something or other breeds company, so I'll admit my own conversation was a bit closer in tone to what I was hearing, not trying to match her, but just being friendly. She claimed to be a graduate of a small Jesuit Liberal Arts College in the East, so we had that in common for openers. Claimed she was working as a fundraiser for an NGO in Guiné Bissau in West Africa, so there was a bit of a Portuguese connection as well. I explained my long-standing connection to

Brazil and that I was a prof at U. of Nebraska. She claimed her husband was "in" with the big-time documentary film makers in New York and would really be interested in my project, so she gave me what turned out to be an unanswerable email address. The conversation was hilarious as the evening proceeded; she managed to describe and berate all the Jesuit profs at her school (names unmentioned, you guess), told of some she had sex with, and described a life a whole lot more interesting than mine. We did agree that the Jesuits were good educators (day time job) and that God is good. I bought her a couple of beers and was on the verge of seeing what else might happen when conscience and good sense and maybe being too stupid to see a good opportunity brought me to slide off the bar stool, saying it had been stimulating and escaping out the door to the hotel. Oh, in the course of our conversation, she said, she was waiting to meet someone. Whoever it was never showed up before I left. Gaherty, you stupid asshole! You can take the boy out of the country ...

The next morning, I did the "early bird" checkout, walked the two blocks to the trains and four hours later was in D.C. I called Molly's number (we had written each other and planned on the meeting days before). I was really dreading this conversation and I guess the tone of my voice showed it. Instead of meeting at her apartment we decided on neutral ground at one of our favorite old hangouts, the Dubliner down from Capitol Hill. I had figured on bunking on her divan since my flight out to Lincoln was not until the next morning; that remained to be seen.

We met just inside the entrance to the bar; she looked ravishing with that auburn hair, beautiful green eyes and of course the stylish figure. We exchanged a tentative kiss, embrace and found a quiet booth in the back where it was not so loud. It was Molly who had introduced me to the place back in 1967 when I returned to D.C. to try to write the dissertation and our love really bloomed from that point on up to the past June when I described the departure for Brazil. After a few pleasantries of "How have you been doing, how was the flight, and I'm relieved you are safe (we hear bad things about events in Brazil)," she said one word: "So?"

I took a deep breath and related a short version of the three months in Brazil. Molly said she had kept up with the "Letters" in the "Times" and had paid close attention to my visits to the Ferreira household, the talks and meeting Cristina Maria (this was all in the "business" version in "Letters," certainly not the torrid times in the Castelinho and the motel). She was encouraged by the publication agreements (one step closer to tenure and our possible future?). The fun ended when I had to tell her the Gaherty Irish honest version of where things stood – that I still had deep feelings for Cristina Maria and her for me, that she was instrumental in the possible research for 1970, but that there were no plans beyond that. None of this would have mattered if I had not expressed Cristina Maria's role.

"Well Mike, I guess this puts us and me on hold another goddamed year! I really thought you loved me, cared for me and wanted me as part of your future, but, crap! I'm not about to be put off yet again. This romance is cooling faster than the lousy warm beer in this place. For your information, I have not been cooling my feet waiting alone here either, hunkered down in the apartment. You know that nice Jewish guy I dated before we met, the one with all the great connections to collecting those blues recordings from the old masters in Mississippi? He loves me, does not mind I'm not Jewish, and by the way his family is loaded, so what matters is love. Nothing else. And besides, his family has connections to that medical book company where I've been working since graduation in 1967. But what I really want to know is did you fuck her? For some stupid reason I kept us restrained along that line even though I really wanted to several times, and there were some close calls when you slept over at the apartment. So what about it?"

The old, worn out clichés from the innocent 60s flashed through my mind, "Yeah, but it was just the hormones and the sex, a one-nighter and no love involved." Except that wasn't exactly true. I'm a lousy liar, all that bullshit Catholic morality and sin and the fires of hell we were raised on. And besides, goddammit, I myself was still not sure about the two of them. So, I said, "All I can tell you is that we're planning on the research for 1970, she's an integral part of the connections I need, and yes, I still care for her. The truth now is the same as I told her in Rio: I'm an American first, as corny as that is, but also true, and I could never immigrate to Brazil and spend my life there, no matter what. And she by the way wants no part of the U.S. So, any future marriage or living there is out of the question. You can chew on that for a while. And I still love you."

Molly sat for a moment, her face turning a bit flushed, picked up her sweater and purse, and headed for the door, but not before her last words: "You fucked her, I know you did. And you may be in love with her for that matter. I believe your patriotism story and all that, that was never a mystery to me. But I'm thinking what if we were to get married, have kids, me being a good professor's wife in Lincoln, and you heading down to Brazil every summer or so for another romp in the hay with your hot Brazilian sweetie? That my friend will never happen! Maybe she will get caught in a revolution in that crazy place, or start one, and it sounds like she has good possibilities of her own. So, let's roll the dice. I'm so pissed off now I can't talk about it. And I'm not leaving Sherman either. I do give you permission to call me in six months and we'll see what's new. I won't say 'You'll regret this,' but I sure as hell say, 'You have missed the boat.' With that she stormed out of the Dubliner and my life, or at least for a while.

18

ALL'S WELL IN LINCOLN, NOT IN BRAZIL

After NOT sleeping on Molly's divan, the next morning, I caught the train to Dulles, then the four-hour flight to Omaha, and the short hop to Lincoln. I was emotionally exhausted and just needed a couple of days to "decompress" from Rio, New York and Washington. I checked in at the Language-Literature Department, made an appointment with my boss Dr. Hillardson to review the summer, and began to furiously get my course outlines, manuals and notes together to be in the classroom in a week. I would be doing a Spanish Survey of Literature course, a Brazilian Survey course and basic Portuguese. I sent off the final draft of the last "Letter" and awaited developments.

Dr. Hillardson, that rarity yet in 1969, an Anglo but with a Ph.D. in Spanish and a true love for such things, not so different from me, welcomed me into his office the next Monday morning. He wondered how it had all gone in Brazil and was pleased when I told him of the agreement for the small book in Recife and the research article at the Folklore Institute in Rio. He said, "Seems to me you are really on the right track. Congratulations! I don't know have too much personal experience with Brazil, but from what you say, you've got the right connections. Mike, we're 'on the make' here and the more you can produce, the better for you and us. Good work."

I thanked the good Dr. and told him of the plans for 1970, all with the "blessing" of James Hansen at the NYT. He practically gushed, such big city publicity was what U of N thrived on. Once again, "Good work. Keep me posted throughout the year and we'll see what I can do for you in May."

As ill winds would have it, leaving his office which was connected to the main office of the LL department, I ran into Professor Miller, the Full Professor of Spanish and "boy wonder" at the Language and Literature Department of U of N. He said, "I heard you were back in Brazil working on that 'para-literature' or whatever it is; you know it's really at the bottom of the barrel when it comes to any 'serious' research. That kind of shit should not really be involved in the academy, and those of us in real literary criticism and teaching of literature know it. I'm not sure how all that will pan out when it comes to tenure time."

I wanted to punch him out right there, notwithstanding the place – the main office of my work. "Professor Miller, we've had a bit of this conversation before. I know you don't give a shit for what I'm doing or even for the major writers associated with it, but a book at the University of Pernambuco Press and an article at the major entity for Brazilian Folklore are not bad for openers."

"We'll see. We'll see," was his response.

I would theoretically have to deal with that s.o.b. for the next ten years through tenure and up the ranks to Full Professor. Good thing I was not particularly confrontational. He still needed to be punched out.

That Fall of 1969 moved along rapidly, me mainly being immersed in classes, "sponsoring" the L & L Brazil Club, doing the Friday p.m. pizza and beer get – togethers with the Portuguese students, and seeing a couple of Big Red football games, notably the one when we squeaked by Oklahoma on a late "Hail Mary" pass. The bedlam that ensued was worth the price of admission, both of us major contenders for the title in the Big 8 Conference.

Later that Fall came major news from Brazil. Another big moment in the political odyssey would take place. General Garrastazu Médici was "elected" to replace General Costa e Silva in October of 1969. His government would be that of the "censura prévia" ["prior censorship"], of AI -5, terrorism, torture and imprisonment.

Major among many items was the kidnapping of U.S. Ambassador Elbrick by the fragmented left in Brazil. Fernando Gabeira, of book fame for his "O Que É Isso, Companheiro?" ["What's This, Comrade?"] was instrumental in the moment. They cornered Elbrick's limousine in traffic, cut it off, threatened the driver, tied up Elbrick and threw him in the back of the limo and drove away like crazy; they later ditched the limo and moved Elbrick to the rear of a VW Kombi. They drove for about two hours up into the hills outside of Rio and when they began to interrogate him, he mistakenly resisted (he was only 57 days in the country and still had not been briefed thoroughly and really knew nothing). The result was a severe beating about the head (it took 75 stitches to sew up, Elbrick was never the same years later). They kept him four days, giving him little food and a Ho Chi Minh book for reading.

The guards were young students just following orders; they really knew little about Elbrick or the movement behind the kidnapping. President Nixon refused to intervene, not wanting anything to do with Brazilian terrorism or to offend his military allies. But the generals for whatever reason ceded to the revolutionaries' demands – liberating fifteen political prisoners. Elbrick was released but it marked a new high in the tense political atmosphere in Brazil. It would be just the beginning of an acceleration by the left in terrorism, the kidnapping of the Japanese ambassador later that year and a series of bank robberies to raise funds.

A major event involved Carlos Marighella and the terrorist activities already described. He was killed by the police on the 4th of November 1969. He was the Brazilian "guru" of urban guerrilla warfare known for his "Mini-Manual of the Urban Guerrilla." He had been a long-time activist in the Communist Party of Brazil with links to Russia and eventually Cuba. Arrested many times, imprisoned, pardoned, arrested again, at the end of his life he had founded the ALN ("Aliança Libertadora Nacional) in 1968; it was members of the ALN that had kidnapped Elbrick. Active in terrorism in greater São Paulo with bank robberies and kidnappings, he was ambushed in that city and killed by the police.

Related to Chico Buarque and family still back in Italy, Chico's friend Toquinho said in November 1969 he himself had to return to Brazil and as a gift, gave melody and some lyrics of "Samba de Orly" to Chico. Chico finished it. Vinicius de Morais added verses, censors objected, and they redid the final lyrics.

Old friend and Brazilian cultural "heavy weight" Vinicius de Morais gave Chico the "jeito" of how to return to Brazil. (The Phillips Recording Company executive assured them "Things are getting better in Brazil.") Chico returned in a blitz of shows, his 4th LP with the hits "Minha Historia" and "Valsinha." But Phillips' optimism was false: Chico was condemned by the press for returning – indicating "he had accepted the dictatorship," all this in March 1970.

Such were the events and atmosphere at the end of 1969 and early 1970 with the intensification of both subversion and military oppression in Brazil. But I was still determined to apply for a grant, in this case to the American Philosophical Society in Philadelphia and go to Brazil in the summer of 1970 to see if the "Chico Buarque" plan would work out. I used all that information already seen in my narrative plus a lot more garnered in those months in Lincoln. I thought that if James Hansen wrote a letter of recommendation, the grant would be "in the bag," and after a busy year in academia I would be ready to return to Rio in June of 1970.

19

LONELY IN ACADEMIA, DEVELOPMENTS IN D.C.

However, closer to home there were personal events to come. I was lonely as hell in Lincoln and in spite of an incident during office hours when this stacked, beautiful Latina student announced "I'll do anything for an A" in my Portuguese language class (I listened, admired her looks but wisely gently counseled more study; crap, they could crucify you in academia for making a wrong move like that, especially in your office during office hours!). Thoughts returned to Molly in D.C. So I made the phone call during semester break. It was much more than being horny; it was loneliness and fond memories of our times in Washington during graduate school. And I thought we were meant for each other. For whatever reason she decided to talk to me and even patiently explained that she was doing all right, still seeing Sherman, but was not so sure that she being Catholic and he Jewish (although not Orthodox) that things would work out. At the time we both were still staunch Catholics if not exactly candidates for sainthood. I said I really wanted to see her and offered to fly to D.C. for a week during the break and we could get to know each other again.

In D.C. it was like old times, we renewed the relationship and really got on well. There was a trip back to the Dubliner where Molly had introduced me to Irish music in that famous bar-restaurant down the hill from the Capitol, a visit to the Corcoran Gallery and the National Art Museum and lots of talk, lots. I reiterated that there was no way I could live permanently in Brazil and that Cristina Maria would have nothing to do with the U.S, and finally that our only agreement was the research for 1970 with her instrumental in introducing me to Chico Buarque. And I perhaps foolishly admitted to the one-time "fling" with Cristina at the Motel in Rio, hoping to clear the air and start with a clean slate. Molly wanted details; she got few. Molly knew of my escapades with Latino friends at whorehouses in Mexico and Brazil for that matter – not the least my unlucky episode with the "clap" in 1967 and all the ramifications. So she knew how bachelor hormones in Latin America were taken care of.

"This is different. You told me last summer that you had to decide between Cristina Maria and me. Apparently, the sex was good, although I'm sure you've only told me part of the story. I can't commit to you or even love you if I thought that would happen again. Your macho relief with the whores, okay. I'll chalk that off to normal hormones and guys who get horny, and I know enough about Latino ways that you were doing what all the guys were doing and that it's the 'system' down there. I'm not so sure what the emotions are – do you love her? If we are to even think of the future, you have to swear to me, as a good Catholic, that even though we are not married, you would not be 'unfaithful.' Can you do that? Or is there going to be a repeat of this past summer? Mike, I can't wait forever or be made a fool of."

I swore I could, but I had to remind her that I had never asked her similar questions and she was silent as a stone about her own doings. Her response, "I may have smoked some dope with the blues crowd but there was never any sex. I am as pure as the winter snow!" Result - we slept together that night, cuddling if you will, but no sex. There was a teary goodbye the next day at Dulles with both of us saying this was a new beginning, and she promising to meet me in Lincoln later in the Spring, mainly to see if we still felt the same. Molly in all her beauty and charm seemed to be the girl for me.

20
MOLLY'S VISIT

That's the way it turned out after a cold and snowy winter in Lincoln and the humdrum business of teaching classes, mainly a continuation of what I had been doing in the Fall Term. Molly and I decided her visit should come during "spring" break in the middle of March, mainly because I would have a week off. I picked her up at the airport in Omaha and we drove in my new Chevy Malibu to Lincoln; she would bunk at my one-bedroom apartment just off the U of N campus, sleeping incidentally on the divan in the living room.

In Lincoln if you don't want to spend the day looking at corn pickers and John Deere tractors, there is not a helluva lot to see other than the campus itself, that is, with one big exception. In March there is the largest gathering of Sand Hill Cranes in all the U.S. out along the Platt River in central Nebraska, by general estimates one million birds! I don't know how much each one needs to eat each day but suffice to say the Nebraska farmers (paid at that) save corn and other grains in harvest fields to keep their gullets full. I think there is some subsidy by the State because thousands of tourists and bird lovers come for the spectacle. We could see it all in a day trip, a long day to be sure. You have to be there early in the morning when they all take off to feed along a hundred miles of river, and more impressive, the late afternoon "fly in" which is a beautiful spectacle of them gliding back in to socialize and spend the night. Only one other minor problem, it's the worst time of year for Nebraska weather – generally freezing temperatures and a combination of hail, sleet and cold rain. Anyway, we got up at 4:00 a.m. did the two-hour drive, spent the day with all the cackling, jumping up and down (the male's mating routine, a real hoot) and dodging National Geographic photographers with their two-foot-long cameras and tri-pods.

Back at home in Lincoln, we warmed up in a Cornhusker Bar with drinks and chicken fried steak, potatoes and gravy and retired to the apartment for more serious stuff. In a moment of I don't know what I proposed to Molly. There was an immediate "yes" (maybe a surprise to the readers) and we in effect "consummated" the deal that evening in my bedroom. I'll not go into details other than that it was a "Catholic" thing with both of our promises of love, fidelity and in a way a return to the values of our upbringing. Great happiness and setting the date for a wedding back in D.C. during semester break of the next school year. There of course was an understanding that ole' Mike would abide by previous promises of fidelity to my American – Irish lass.

I ask myself, was all this as described a "lesser" moment than that motel in Rio? Not in terms of truthfulness and our future. And even the sex. Molly was as passionate as one might imagine, and we were a good fit. Oh. I might as well say it now, that winter, after Molly's visit, in correspondence with Cristina before heading back to Brazil, she informed me that we would be life-long friends, but she too had made a decision – to accept marriage to a long-time suitor, friend of the Ferreira family, of the "right" social class and economic standing, and a postscript saying he would join the family firm. But this would not stop our commitment to research plans and the project with Chico; it was all stated prosaically for a Brazilian, but in effect both of just getting our "ducks in a row."

So from Sand Hill Cranes to ducks, it all came to pass.

21

GREEN LIGHT FOR BRAZIL

Sure enough, the American Philosophical Society liked my summer grant proposal (with James Hansen's letter along with three others by university professors, my nemesis Professor Miller not among them) and came through with its prestige if not big dollars. It was $2000, enough for minimal careful budgeting in Recife and Rio. Stingy but "on the make" U of N chipped in $1000 for the airline ticket and air travel in Brazil. I would go to Recife first, checking out "Cordel" production there, but also with a visit to the University Press of Pernambuco (and Ariano Suassuna) this because the promised book had failed to materialize. Uh oh!

Good news came from New York and Washington. James Hansen wanted the return to "Letters," reiterating that 1969 was good in the Sunday editions, but not yet enough for another book. And good ole' Iverson of the INR – WHA agreed on the diplomatic-journalist visa. We were all cognizant of the late changes in 1969 with the ever-worsening dictatorship and opposition violence, this in the Garrastazu Médici regime. It was all the more important for my reporting, albeit with advice for a much greater degree of caution on my part. I would receive small stipends from both, easing the pain and worries for dealing with the rampant inflation and economic unrest in Brazil. Soon enough I and the readers would be awakened to all that.

Long phone calls to Molly in Washington, you might say our AT&T "love letters," my promise to write often from Brazil, and a "not to worry" about the wedding; Molly and her Mom would handle all that, and fine with me.

PART II

BRAZIL 1970

EPIGRAPH

"Pedro Pedreiro, Penseiro, Esperando o Trem ..." (Chico Buarque de Hollanda)
"Pete the Laborer, Thinking, Waiting for the Train ..."

"Apesar de você ..." (Chico Buarque de Hollanda)
"In Spite of You"

1

FLOODS, "BUGS," ARIANO AND GEROALDO

With the atmosphere of terrorism against the military regime now in Brazil in 1970 - the sequesters of businessmen and even diplomats, and bombs thrown at banks and the like, there was a huge change in the security at airports, passenger and luggage checks. The introduction for me was at the airport of Belém do Paraá where I entered Brazil on my way to Recife, Pernambuco, my first destination (the reader may recall I did the same route in 1969). After spending the night at a very modest hotel on Avenida Getúlio Vargas in Belém, I got up at 4:00 a.m., arrived at the Belém airport at 5:00 a.m., and my flight left for Recife at 8:30 a.m. due to all the security restrictions of the DOPS. The delay was due to a body search – a "personal" search of the entire body! And they were thorough.

There was a repeat of the "machismo" and the "esprit de corps" of Brazilian airline pilots that morning. At the end of the flight from Belém we were arriving at our destination of the Guararapes International Airport in Recife but with unstable weather and heavy thunderstorms. Upon entering the flight pattern for landing, the airplane descending rapidly and precipitously, at the moment the wheels should have made contact with the tarmac, the plane suddenly surged upward, gaining in velocity. Looking out the small window, I noticed that the landing strip was well to the left of our flight path. Then the pilot pulled the "Emerson Fittipaldi" Indianapolis 500 maneuver: he "goosed" the engines, climbed at g-level speed and veered the airplane sharply to the left. All of us were suddenly flying over the Atlantic Ocean! Then the airplane circled, and we landed on the proper runway, this on our second try. No

North American pilot would dare to undertake the abrupt maneuvers we had just witnessed on the Varig.

In Recife I was staying in the home of old friend Fábio Heráclio who now was in São Paulo doing graduate work in engineering (he of the close call with the DOPS at the Recife docks in 1969). His brother Gastão with his recent diploma in medicine was a guide. As always in the month of June (like in 1966, 1967 and 1969) it was "winter" in Pernambuco and heavy tropical rains brought serious flooding to the city. The flooded streets were the result of the "blowout" of all three rivers running into this "Venice of Brazil" as a result of the rains in the interior of the Northeast. Gastão, driving us around the city, came to a street with high water, didn't hesitate for a moment and floorboarded it directly into the water. His explanation: "VW Bugs ["Fuscas"] float!" In his defense I think we did float just a bit. In the U.S. there would have been a barrier barring entrance to the street. The Brazilians knew better.

I was only going to be in Recife a few days, so it was "down to business." Rather than take the long bus ride to University City (or the $$ cab ride), I gambled on catching Ariano Suassuna at his former post of head of the State of Pernambuco Department of Culture near the old Law School, familiar territory to me. As luck would have it, he was still there and welcomed me into his office. There was a writer from Peru there as well and was reporting that the biggest play performed in Lima at that time was Ariano's "The Rogues' Trial" ["Auto da Compadecida" – the play I dealt with in the dissertation]. The Peruvian said the script was from a translation in Spanish from an English version – did this reflect that age-old problem of lack of linguistic cooperation or even interest between Portuguese and Spanish learners in South America? Both sides say they can understand perfectly the other's language and speak it as well. Ha! Ariano just laughed and said he had seen terrible translations of his originals even from French and if he sat and worried about all that he would never have time for writing!

When I delicately (carefully) brought up the problem of my so-far-unpublished book, he said, "Miguel, I thought you knew Brazil better than that? It's slow motion down here, and we have to deal with local bigwigs who write their books and pay for their publication, so it boils down to 'first come, first serve.' Politics and social standing play no small role. But don't worry, I went over your Portuguese, and the book is all set; it should come out soon." What could I say, so I said, "Ótimo! I'll be looking forward to that." But my brain was saying, "Nossa! I sure as hell hope so."

After some chit-chat (Ariano had a line of people in the waiting room, all wanting favors), we had the cordial "abraço" and both promised to keep in touch. Letters in the post office on a good day took one week between Lincoln and Brazil (remember: "air mail and registered"), so "não há problema." There was one problem; I had previous ample evidence that Brazilians just don't write letters. There was really nothing left to be done in Recife, so I set up the flight down to Rio for the next day.

I can't leave Pernambuco without telling the reader, that sure enough, my "old friend" Neroaldo of the Recife DOPS greeted me at the check-in counter of Varig, he of past "scrapes" in 1967 and 1969.

Dressed in the usual white linen suit for the tropics, wrinkled as usual from the humidity, and a thin black tie, with a jaunty straw hat "fedora style," he gave me a big smile, that familiar embrace and fairly jabbered on for about ten minutes, this after assuring me we had time for a "cafezinho" before they called the flight. His news, although not a surprise, was a little disturbing and what I hoped was not a portent for things to come.

"Mike, welcome back to Brazil and Recife; we've been expecting you. You did good work last year, although reporting on those shithead poems of 'Cordel' in my opinion is not high on the list of important things in Brazil, but so be it. I'm in close touch with our mutual friend in Rio, Heitor Dias, so we are up to date. I note you were with Suassuna again; his movie was approved later last year and did great at the box office, and he's an 'icon' untouchable, so far, in Pernambuco, so no harm done. I hope your book comes out, but don't hold your breath with the UPE press.

"Moving on to other matters, you know all that's happened since you were last with us last August. Garrastazu Médici is now in control of things, there are more kidnappings and bank robberies, but AI – 5 now is in full force. The left, especially the students, are now under constant surveillance, and we've had to shut down that 'liberal' University in Brasília. I've got it from Heitor you will be with that Cristina Maria, daughter of the nasty leftist ex-congressman in Rio, and that you may be trying to get in touch with Chico Buarque. That's a dumb choice. All this with your 'protected' visa and passport from INR-WHA. So, we'll see how your research and reporting go. You know that Chico whom I admire for his old songs like 'a Banda' and nice sambas has another side, and that he was 'asked' to leave Brazil after that famous 'Passeata dos Cem Mil' ['100,000 Demonstration']. We still don't have any proof he's a Commie, but he stole that car in São Paulo when he was 19 years old and was in jail a night or two until his friends used some 'pistolão' [political pull] to get him out. For sure he is mixed up with the Left, so I'm not really sure what the hell you are up to getting involved with him. My simple counsel: be careful!"

I retorted, "Geroaldo, I think I may know more about this than you. Sure, he basically is pro-democracy, and was always against the military takeover, like a few million other Brazilians. But, 'merda,' he was excoriated by the Left for not joining them in leftist actions, and only joined the 'Passeata dos Cem Mil' for his own safety from them. He damned near starved to death in exile in Rome, trying to take care of his wife Marieta and their baby, losing out on his savings and business interests back home in Rio, and it's only through Vinicius de Morais' advice that he's even back in Brazil. Friends in high places. You'll see, my only interest with Chico is sharing my research, our common interest in the Northeast (he did the music to that great 'Auto de Natal' ['Christmas Play'] from João Cabral de Melo Neto, 'Morte e Vida Severina' a work of genius, but my connection will be to the song 'Pedro Pedreiro' he did even before the Revolution. Both pieces have to do with one of the major themes of 'Cordel,' the migration from the 'sertão' and hunger and death searching for a better life in Recife and then south to Rio de Janeiro. Do you know that song?"

"Hell no. But you can be sure I'll check it out now. Mike, we're almost friends and I think still on the same side, so keep your nose clean okay?"

"Geroaldo, just a personal aside. Chico 'lifted' that car as a teenage prank and has always been an idealist. Weren't you ever in trouble as a teenager or in your twenties? I got in trouble in Lincoln in high school when we got a bit drunk and drove over the high school principal's lawn and got hauled down to the police station. Puta que pariu!"

"Mike, I like you better each time we talk. You know some Portuguese! Sure, we pulled a lot of shit back in my home town of Garanhuns in the interior, and there were some fights in bars, including one time when this punk pulled a knife on me and I grabbed it and beat the shit out of him. The only bad news was he was a relative of the local political chief 'coronel,' and I was on the wrong side. He was drunk at the time and a friend of my Dad's, a local politico, smoothed over the whole thing. Oh yeah, and I roughed up a couple of whores in the local cabaret when they tried to screw me (pardon the pun) – charge me double for a blow job. But I'm a patriot, served in the national guard with exemplary duty, did some good police detective work in the police force in Recife and got this job. The point is, I'm on the right side now, and hope you are. I'll pay for the 'cafezinho' and pass this conversation on down to Heitor. By the way, I know of your escapades in the zone in Boa Viagem so we have something in common, I mean the whores you know."

"Enough said. Geroaldo, we should put this all under our hat and hope for better times. The whole deal with Chico is still a dream; I'm not in touch with him yet." We said goodbye and I got on the Varig flight to Rio. For now, anyway, I was out of the clutches of the DOPS in Recife.

2

ROMANCE IN RIO RESOLVED

We arrived at the Galeão in Rio amidst the usual smog and fog and I took the "frescão" down to the Santos Dumont downtown "shuttle" airport, a far cheaper ride than the taxi from the Ilha do Governador and the big airport. I took a chance and took a taxi to Dona Júlia's boarding house in Copacabana, and luck would have it, first, she was still kicking, and second, accepting boarders. We were friends from times before, so I moved in and prepared for what was to come. Ole' Júlia, feisty as ever began swearing immediately (she had a vocabulary matching most men in Brazil) at those "cafajestes" [s.o.b.s] running the country, noting that the first military president from her home state of Ceará was long gone, as was his successor General Costa e Silva and now Brazil was dealing with full blown suppression and oppression. She seemed to have no fear about talking about it in the privacy of her living room.

I was nervous for the first encounter with Cristina Maria, taking into consideration her news about the upcoming marriage, but also my "new" situation with Molly. I was banking on the fact that none of this would interfere with our agreement from 1969 to proceed with the project and proposal toChico Buarque but was also nervous about exactly what the reception would be at her parents' house. I made the call and her voice over the phone was neutral enough, non-committal as to either her or my personal lives but making the invitation to come over the next night, see her family again and promising to talk about project plans.

The time came. I rang the doorbell and a gorgeous, fully blossomed young lady answered me at the door. If possible, she seemed more beautiful than ever before. She was dressed modestly, but that voluptuous figure was not hidden by the tight blouse and skirt. There was the quick "abraço" and kiss on the cheek, a big smile but not the close touching of her body against mine like in '69. Men remember such things. I was ushered into the living room, and once again most everyone was there, Jaime, his wife Dona Regina, but not the now high school age brothers out with their busy lives. Both the parents greeted me warmly saying they were glad to see me once again. Jaime offered me a before dinner drink ["aperitivo"], and a conversation began.

There was the expected chit-chat of getting caught up on all our lives the past year. I filled them in on academic matters at the University, small city life in Lincoln, and the recent conversation with Ariano Suassuna in Recife. No need to mention Geroaldo. I also told him the connection to the "Times" and INR-WHA was still in place, but I did not mention Molly. There might be a time later for that.

Jaime basically told me of all the political developments, most of which I've already mentioned in the preface to "1970." He was rather glum about it all, noting more colleagues from his time in congress, were, like him, on the "list" of the DOPS and one or two, in particular from MEB [Base Educational Movement] days in Recife, had left the country.

"So far, aside from tailing me and a wire on the phones here, they have let me continue with business affairs, once again, as long as I have the 'right' customers. They are pro-business and my connections in Pará and Amazonas are in line with national development plans for the region. I'm sure they have a close watch as well on my bank accounts (no deposits of funds outside Brazil, hypocrisy in itself since they are all filling their pockets and doing a nice correspondence with the banks in Switzerland); I'm only allowed to travel to acceptable business connections, conferences and the like, and none outside of Brazil. So life goes on, business is good, and I'm certainly not making any political announcements. I've got a family to take care, and we both want all the kids to get a good education, so right now those are the options.

"Cristina tells me you know of her developments; Otávio her 'noivo' [fiancé] is the son of a long-time business associate, is a good kid and will fit well into the business; he's a natural at marketing and carries himself well. Both Regina and I are happy about it all, but I have to tell you, there are some mixed emotions. We thought and still think the world of you and would not have been at all disappointed if things with you and Cristina had worked out. She explained your reticence about moving to Brazil for the long term. In spite of all the nonsense going on here, I still love my country and certainly can understand why you would not want to cut ties with yours. We don't see any of this as a problem with your 'joint' proposal for Chico Buarque; Cristina has given us some details.

It was my turn again.

"Jaime, Regina and Cristina. You have 'hit the nail on the head.' The reality is what you just have described, so all I am hoping is to keep things on a 'business' relationship and hopefully have a successful project these months. We'll definitely keep you posted on progress."

On that note, Cristina and I repaired once again to the Castelinho for some serious talk. I'm telling the reader to not expect a repeat of last year, and it was not. Sort of. There was the minor detail, not so minor, of our even going out alone, thinking of Otávio and consequences. Cristina assured me he was a gentleman, understood our arrangement, and as long as there was no funny business, he was cool with it, saying he did not have to come along to check. We walked the short way, found our old booth in the back, order two "choppes" and made some plans. There was no kissing, no fondling, but the eyes are the window of the soul, and I still saw in her eyes that the memories of 1969 had not gone away. "Rapaz," it was difficult. For both of us.

Cristina said, "I've already contacted Chico and Marieta and made some arrangements, mainly telling them you are a serious researcher and it all would be good for his career and image as well – working with a U.S. college professor with ties to INR-WHA – and besides I thought you both would have lots to talk about. Chico agreed to have us both come to the house in Laranjeiras next week. I'll let you know the day and time. Get your ducks in a row; Chico is a busy person. If he takes a liking to you, and that's not a given, I think you will have some success.

"Mike, I want you to know that I think both you and I have made the right decisions. Molly sounds great and will fit your future. In my case, Otávio has always been a dream, although I will admit the job with Dad's company may have swayed him a bit in proposing. It isn't like it is a 'fixed marriage,' we love each other. I'm looking forward to having him meet you; I think you both can handle it. I have not forgotten our great times together and wish things could have progressed, but we certainly had our fun. By the way, Otávio does not know about the motel. I'm sure you can keep that quiet. He knows about you but not introducing you would make things a bit unwieldy. Or not?"

"I'm not so sure about that. We still in a sense are or at least were rivals for your affection, and I know Brazilian men. Just see what he says, asks and all in coming days. Once you introduce me to Chico, I can take it from there and maybe just give you a report in a month or two, so there won't be any need to be with you, and he in turn won't have to wonder. What do you think?"

"Uh, I'm not so sure, but we can try it. I'll call you next week when I've got the date with Chico."

3

ROUTINE IN RIO

In the interim I managed to keep busy, some of the time with Americans who came back into the picture, some with some interesting research developments. One was getting back with touch with Steve Baldini of Recife and Rio days in both 1967 and 1969. He was now an executive with CARITAS in Rio, a perfect fit for both his educational preparation at Harvard and his Catholic social consciousness. With an apartment in Ipanema, modest to be sure, and a nice car provided to him by the company, he took me around town some and introduced me to some interesting people, and by the way, new Brazilian customs, the latter important for "Letters."

One such occasion was meeting the Lawrence family and visiting their lavish apartment in Parque Guinle with its distant view to the Bay of Guanabara (Larry was the representative of the Library of Congress in Brazil, with duty formerly in several African countries). An aside: Jorguinho Guinle in those days was perhaps <u>the</u> playboy about town in Rio. The family not only owned the Copacabana Palace Hotel but the prime real estate in all Rio that would become Parque Guinle. The old president's mansion (before Brasília) was there. A professional aside: Larry in his capacity as Library of Congress Director in Brazil happened to see my book on a list of future publications for the University Press of Pernambuco, a good sign for the future. He was most hospitable and kind. Steve was good friends with the family, including the two daughters, and we all had a fun night at that nightclub "Berro DÁgua" high above the Lagoa, the same place I had taken Cristina in 1969.

There was one more curious note about Steve and an essential note to my next "Letter" to the "Times" - A Brazilian Institution: the "Despachante."

The "dispatcher" or "despachante" is a person or agent who is hired to "cut through" the terrible red tape and bureaucracy of Brazilian life. Steve showed me what seemed to have been a two-inch thick billfold full of the documents needed for him to simply leave Brazil, go to New York City, marry his fiancée and bring her back to Brazil to live with him, as husband and wife. Steve, a veteran of things Brazilian if there ever was one, was finally forced by inaction and exasperation to hire a "despachante" who was ever so slowly getting through the process.

Of all sources to know about the "despachante," one of the best is by novelist John Grisham in his novel taking place in Brazil called "The Testament." Grisham writes (fiction of course, but not far from reality), "No official document is obtained in Brazil with waiting in long lines. The "despachante" knows the city clerks, the courthouse crowd, the politicians, and the customs agents. He knows the system and how to grease it to get things done. The job requires a quick tongue, patience and a lot of brass." (Quoted by Robert de Paolo in "Doing Business in Brazil").

This is a professionalized example of the "jeito," the source of such things. It means finding a way to get around something, a law, a custom, a rule, and all done in good faith with all parties satisfied.

And there was continued "Cordel" research and reading at the old Casa de Rui Barbosa in Botafogo. On different occasions there I met for the first time the great Théo Brandão, folklorist from Alagoas and in my view the second best in all Brazil, following only Luís da Câmara Cascudo in Natal. He had seen my article in the "Revista Brasileira de Folclore" and was now deep in research on the classic poem of "Cordel," "The Gambling Soldier," ("O Soldado Jogador"). It was rather unbelievable to learn that he had 500 manuscript pages written so far and is not finished! That's the story-poem with a theme somehow discovered by T. Texas Tyler who passed it on to Tex Ritter who recorded "Deck of Cards." It's a small world.

On yet another time while reading the story-poems at the Casa I met the "Cordel" poet and publisher Joaquim Batista de Sena from Fortaleza, Ceará, a relative of Sebastião Nunes Batista, my "man" at the Casa. The encounter took place in the library of the Casa de Rui Barbosa and was a pleasure; Joaquim was a major figure in northeastern "Cordel" in the 1950s and 1960s. Upon his death his works and stock of "Cordel" would be obtained by Manoel Caboclo e Silva in Juazeiro do Norte.

Just as important, it those days I saw the seminal black and white documentary film by Tânia Quaresma on "Cordel" and the folklore of the Northeast. It was a "classic" from the 1960s with the scenes of poet-singers ("cantadores"), the northeastern cowboys in their outfits of leather from head to toe, scenes from the Cariri region of Ceará (the land of Father Cícero and the "holy women" of Juazeiro), and Father

Cícero's successor Friar Damian. It was one of the first efforts to capture that amazing folkloric scene of the Northeast on film, albeit in the black and white of the times.

And finally, I met for the first time the ubiquitous and famous professor from the Sorbonne, Raymond Cantel; he would really put "Cordel" on the map in Brazil with his interviews with major dailies and weekly news magazines. There is almost a "myth" grown up around this man, both pro and con. He would arrive in Rio or São Paulo on Air France, immediately contact the press basically saying, "I have arrived" and garner the interviews. If you know how Brazilian intellectuals have an infatuation with the Sorbonne and anyone connected to it, it's no surprise. A bit of an intellectual dandy, he also became known for his amazing collection of "Cordel" which he guarded zealously in Portiers, France. He never published much, but certainly did cause intellectuals dragging their feet in Brazil to take notice of the "Cordel." (This folk-popular poetry was truly looked down upon and/or ignored by most of the Brazilian intelligentsia in the 1960s.) When I heard the professor speak on a couple of occasions his papers were incredibly clear, free of jargon and fine work.

And finally, on a personal note (not for "Letters") there was a fine reunion with my first Brazilian friend dating from undergraduate days at Creighton U. in Omaha. Caetano and wife Glória were married at the Igreja do Carmo in the center of Rio with the wedding reception at the Copacabana Palace Hotel and honeymoon in Amsterdam. I stayed with the family in my very first days in Brazil in June of 1966, getting to know Caetano's mother and brother. This was that "other" Brazil of the upper class. Those were sentimental days. Caetano introduced me to Copacabana nightlife, took me to my first Brazilian soccer game, a doozy at the Maracanã, and my first Brazilian "Love," that rosewood Di Giorgio classic guitar was kept in their house while I did fieldwork for six months in the Northeast.

4

A DREAM COME TRUE

After all the above, in late June I got the call from Cristina Maria. It was all set. She would pick me up in the family sedan and we would drive to Laranjeiras and I would finally meet Chico and Marieta. I've got to admit I was really nervous and apprehensive. Here I was finally, after years of admiration and study, getting the chance to meet one of my great Brazilian heroes, and perhaps a key to future research in Brazil. I told her thanks and said to chip in with all the right words. We arrived at the house with a gate in front, and with what seemed like a forest of trees surrounding the entire place, many I think "mangueira," pushed the buzzer on the gate, and a "porteiro" came, opened it and let us in.

Before we even got out of the car, I heard a familiar voice (from the recordings) say, "Oi Cristina, faz tempo, bem vindo à casa." It was Chico himself, dressed in one of those plaid shirts from an album cover, looking a bit haggard and thin, but with a big smile. He gave her the big "carioca" embrace and looked me over and said, "You come with a good recommendation. Welcome to the Buarque de Hollanda house. Marieta is out with the kids, so we'll have time to talk without her usual interruptions and questions. Just kidding." I stammered a "Boa Tarde" and followed them into the house, through a large, airy living room with windows open to the garden and back to what must have been Chico's "office" and home recording studio, full of microphones, speakers, three or four nylon string guitars safely propped on their stands, reams and reams of manila folders (music?) and a huge library behind.

Where to begin? He offered a cafezinho calling for the maid and bade us all sit down. He and Cristina reminisced some on high school days with her and Marieta and got right down to business. "Cristina tells me you've got a project that involves me. I hope it's nothing the DOPS will be calling about. I'm on their 'watch' list, and there are strange fellows who patrol the neighborhood. It's like Carlos Drummond de Andrade's famous chronicle when he gets on a first name basic with the thief who assaults him regularly in Copacabana, we know each other and have conversations. No one's banging down the gates, so go ahead and tell me a little about yourself."

I had a prepared list of topics and due to my excitement got them all jumbled and out of order, but, a bit short of breath, managed to give him a ten-minute (that's a long time) introduction. I felt like I was applying for a job as a manager at Phillips Recording Studio.

"Senhor Buarque, Chico, that is, first of all I'm on the list of your admirers, in no small part because Cristina Maria introduced me in 1967 to that first album 'A Banda,' and we watched the MPB Song Festivals on TV at her house. I've followed your career, ups and downs, and music since. But I want you to know a bit about me first." Chico interrupted, saying the "cafezinho" was good but would I like something else, "I'm going to have a "dose" [shot] of "Pitu" myself." I said, "I'm used to the Brahma Choppe from Recife days, do you keep that around the house?" Chico said, "Você deveria estar brincando" ["You must be joking."]." In a flash the maid brought out a big tray with those Styrofoam holders and a couple of big bottles of Brahma. He poured and I talked.

"Chico, I've got a Ph.D. from Georgetown in Spanish and Latin American Studies, and a minor in Luso-Brazilian Studies. I was here for over a year in 1966-1967 doing research for the degree, the topic being your 'literatura de cordel' and erudite Brazilian Literature. I was raised on a small farm in Nebraska, my Dad himself a sort of 'retirante,' [refugee migrant] but middle class, me with Catholic upbringing so I can really relate to the poets, the campesinos and even to the droughts and migration. I'll get down to that later.

He laughed, "Oh yeah, 'a literatura de cordel,' that 'shit' my Uncle Aurélio called 'A literature of little importance.' Well, little he knew, he had never been up to the Feira in São Cristóvão or the Largo de Machado to hear the poets. I did get to the Largo, and even got tipsy a time or two with the poets. 'Pitu' it was. Go on, rapaz."

"Porra, Chico, I'm trying to not take up too much of your time. But I've got to say it was Manuel Cavalcanti Proença, Luís da Câmara Cascudo and Ariano Suasssuna that really helped me this far. And Ariano is backing my book at UFEPE Press 'A Literatura de Cordel.' And the 'Campanha de Folclore' downtown did my first article in Brazil.

"Now I'm back here in Rio still reading 'Cordel' at the Casa de Rui Barbosa, sending my 'chronicles' to the 'New York Times' in monthly 'Letters' and have semi-diplomatic status with the State Department's Institute of Research – Western Hemisphere Analisis. What I hope to write about is any 'Cordel' reflecting current affairs in Brazil plus reporting on the events and people I encounter in Brazil. The latter is where you come in. As you well know, one of the major themes in 'Cordel' is the poverty and struggle to survive in the Northeast, the land holding history (using the 'lavradores' for seasonal work on the sugar cane plantations, the exploitation of the same by the 'coroneis,' and finally driving many off the lands where they were sharecroppers). Where would they go? Thousands did the flight for survival first to Recife and the coast and then more importantly south to Rio and São Paulo where they do menial labor on the construction sites and labor on the farms or drive some of these crazy buses I'm on every day.

"You are probably more aware of all this than most Brazilians. Your phenomenal work on 'Morte e Vida Severina" is closely related to that theme in 'Cordel' but even more so, 'Pedro Pedreiro.' What I basically want to do via interviews is get your 'take' on it all, how you managed to come up with that phenomenal music, but most of all the genesis of 'Pedro Pedreiro.' It's the same theme, coincidentally of Luís Gonzaga's 'Asa Branca' ['White Wing'] which a Russian documentary called the 'anthem of the northeast,' but an entire thematic cycle of 'Cordel." In my research I track the entire story: the poverty and desperation in the Northeast, the flight to the coast, then to the Amazon as rubber gatherers ['seringueiros'] and then mainly to Rio. I've got it all documented in literally dozens of story-poems from 'Cordel;' I want to write in 'Letters' how you in a totally different world came up with the same theme but in your music. Oh, an aside: Cristina's 'connection' to this is having introduced me to your music, her Dad whom you know all about, but also to the MEB [Educational Base Movement] and students of pre – 'redentora' ['redemptive revoluation'] days. The MEB does not appear much in 'Cordel' mainly because the military squelched it, but the 'ABC' folhetos with each strophe a succeeding letter of the alphabet teaching the 'lavradores' to read are a minor part of 'Cordel' and I've documented countless 'nordestinos' who say they learned to read with them, and not just 'lavradores' but middle class folks and students. And the ABC format is everywhere in 'Cordel.'"

Chico was so excited he could hardly talk, a wide grin on his face and some amazement in his eyes, excited to the point he was talking so fast I missed some it and had to ask him to repeat.

"Miguel, this is truly amazing. You are what we call one gringo 'arretado' [a real 'gringo simpático']! Keep your glass full while I react to all this. And Cristina, thank <u>you</u> for getting us together! My visceral reaction is absolutely 'yes,' and you may in fact have inspired me to do a sequel to 'Pedro Pedreiro.' Can you get me copies of all those 'folhetos' telling the 'retirante' story? My explanation to your 'proposta' will take a while. I think we can record it on my 'gravadora' [tape recorder] and you can write it up later. I do reserve rights to read what you write. I want to read your book and all the 'Letters' from last year. I think we have a lot more in common than you might think. It turns out now is better than later because all hell may break loose here in a few weeks because of one of my new songs, but that's another story we can talk about later. And I'm not really sure how easy it will be to get together then."

I said, "Ótimo, fill the glasses, set up your recorder and 'mãos à obra' ['Let's get to work']." I think I was bug-eyed in all my enthusiasm and excitement, first of all just to be in the same room with one of my Brazilian heroes but amazed at my good fortune hearing all this. I won't deny it was not what I had dreamed of, but "Los sueños sueños son" as Calderón de la Barca said in a famous play. This was real life, not a dream.

Chico rummaged in a pile of equipment in the back of the office and soon had the tiny Sony recorder whirring. He said, "Don't worry, I'll supply the tapes; I happen to have a few lying around."

"Miguel (e Cristina), you obviously know 'Morte e Vida Severina' well. Like you, or maybe not, I was just a young naïve and somewhat wild teenager at the time. I had had some success at school parties, 'farra' [singing and partying] in night clubs in São Paulo and a few times on the radio with some early songs. I was just doing my first LP at this same time, and not a coincidence 'Pedro Pedreiro' was the main song. Then out of the blue in 1965 Roberto Freire, the writer and director, came to São Paulo and asked me to put 'Morte e Vida Severina' to music for a play by TUCA (Teatro da Universidade Católica) in São Paulo. I knew the 'Auto de Natal' by João Cabral de Melo Neto (who didn't?) and loved most of all his poetry and the amazing metaphor of the whole thing. (A Gaherty aside: for the reader of "Letters" the play's main character was named "Severino," a very common name for males in the northeast interior, so in one sense the title is life and death of such a person. But "severo" also means "severe" or "difficult" and João Cabral obviously wanted this play on words.) It was an unexpected chance and honor to be asked to do it. I naively said 'yes' right away. Little did I know I was biting off a lot more than I could handle. More on that in a bit. But it was at his house that I sang 'Pedro Pedreiro,' just me and my lousy voice on a Di Giorgio classic guitar. Roberto had a similar reaction to you – was this a coincidence or what? – all that the song and play had in common.

"Anyway, I've got this penchant for putting things off to the last minute or did then; most of the music got done I'm sorry to say after 24 hours straight in the closed off dining room of the family house in São Paulo with one guitar and two big bottles of Pitú to the side. The play got finished and had incredible success in São Paulo and then at an international theater festival in Nancy, France and finally Paris. It was there I finally actually met João Cabral and received his thanks, but for me that whole 'turné' was work and party.

"Most important to me, you know the story-line of the play: a migrant ['retirante'] follows the Capibaribe River in Pernambuco, first a dry river bed in the backlands ['sertão'], then a flowing stream in the 'zona da mata,' the sugar cane plantation area along the coast, and finally to Recife looking to better his life. All he meets are funerals and is finally told by a 'mangue' [tide water slum dweller] in Recife that really, he has been following his own funeral. The story is after all a Christmas story with a new child born and new hope, but that theme of the funeral and especially the song 'Funeral de um Lavrador' were my best contributions.

"Agora, bem," 'Pedro Pedreiro.' It was written a couple of years before 'A Banda' in 1967 and was both on my first LP and also a '45' compact. But it's more; I think when you think about all the lyrics, you'll see it's not quite what you thought – the link to 'Asa Branca' and the flight – migration stories in 'Cordel.' Yet it DOES certainly have a little to do, in part, with that theme. But it's more; we've got time, let me sing it for you.

Chico picked up one of the guitars, tuned it quickly and sang all of "Pedro Pedreiro."

In the song Pedro the northeastern migrant and laborer in São Paulo is waiting for the train, that train that would take him back to the Northeast (in "Cordel" the migrants wait for rain to return to the drought-stricken Northeast, for better crops, so they can go back home). But it's a long wait and his construction job with little pay puts him constantly further behind ("Cordel" has dozens of stories describing this rough life in Rio or São Paulo). Pedro plays the lottery, his only hope for a bigger future and waits for carnival to break the monotony ("Cordel" has an entire thematic cycle on the "jogo do bicho" or national lottery and another on Carnival). And in the song his wife and son wait as well. And just as in "Cordel," Pedro's waiting may never end, and in fact he may die waiting. This is precisely the theme, idea and poignant atmosphere of many of the "Cordel" poems that suggest it's all a pipe dream, that rain will never come, that life in a "favela" may be the end. So why wait? In the end, Chico gives hope, the train is coming! And in some "Cordel" stories, the northeasterner saves some money and does go back "home" to the Northeast.

I was mesmerized by the moment as was Cristina. The incredibly clever lyrics, rhyme, alliterative sounds of the song came home to us. We sat silent for a few moments and then broke into applause. Chico did a "stage bow," put the guitar down, lit a Marlboro and had another shot of cachaça and basically told us the genesis of "Pedro Pedreiro."

"When I was a young kid, still well in my early teens, and a student at a Catholic 'colégio' in São Paulo, the Santa Cruz, I got involved with what amounted to a cult, the 'Ultramontanos;' my buddies and I basically went over the deep end, mainly because of the influence of one of our teachers at the Colégio. We started going to Communion every day, went on absurdly long hikes to mass at their summer camp, and 'nossa!' even gave up 'futebol.' The cult was right out of the Middle Ages and preached the coming end of the world. It turned out later to be related to a Fascist Movement 'Tradition, Family, and Property.' My parents became suspicious and pulled us out of it, a good thing for all.

"But me being from an upper-class family, intellectually and economically, and in a Catholic School, and most buddies in a similar situation, we were still urged to help the poor in any way we could. The vehicle became the 'Organização de Auxílio Fraterno.' We would go, mainly at night, after school, to the center of downtown São Paulo, to places like 'Estação da Luz' and the viaducts in the city. That's where the homeless lived (and still live by the way). We generally brought blankets and clothes, but the strange thing is that they ran from us when we approached. We left all the stuff; it was like feeding a 'feral' cat who would return after you left a bowl of food. Miguel, they were mainly 'nordestinos.' You know somebody said one-third of São Paulo is 'nordestino,' yet they are the most looked down upon and even hated part of the city. I never really got to know any of them on those forays, but those images of them sleeping in the streets and especially under the viaducts never left me. I found myself thinking of them, their life and fate. Everyone knows about the migrations, that most of them work as laborers in construction or maybe even doormen (their wives wash clothes and are maids for rich folks.) Such a couple worked in our house, José e Maria Santos from Paraíba, where else? In Brazil they become 'part of the family,' you know what I mean, not really, but very emotionally linked to the family. We took care of them. Over the years we heard all their story. That became 'Pedro Pedreiro.'"

I said, "Yeah, I agree, it's more than the 'Cordel' stories, but still linked to them. It's deeper, much more profound and incredibly beautiful with the lyrics, the structure and repetitions. Chico, let me think about all this, write up the next 'Letter' and I'll bring it over in about a week; and I'll also get the titles of the story - poems I've been talking about. I don't have the copies, they are all up in Nebraska, but I think all or almost all must be in the Rui Barbosa collection, so I'll do a hunt and xerox what I find. Okay?"

Chico said, "Tá combinado. I've got a better idea, why don't the two of us go to São Cristóvão next Sunday morning to the market. The truth is no one there has heard of Chico Buarque; they like Luís Gonzaga the northeastern country 'forró' singer, but I'll go 'incognito.' I'll pick you up at ten o'clock and we'll check it out. Maybe the titles will be there."

I dared to say, "Chico, if you want the whole experience, we should take the Jardim de Alah bus from the end of Ipanema. I'll take a taxi to your house and we can walk from there. I promise you an adventure. But still best is 'incognito.' I always draw attention; they know a gringo when they see one, and you aren't short enough to be a 'pau de arara;' you don't exactly look the role." He said, "Oh, porra, that's walking distance from the house (I learned later that "walking distance" was a relative term with Chico; it could be three or four miles.) I'll see you next Sunday here, what time?" I said, "They go all day, but let's say 9:00 a.m."

Cristina Maria dropped me off at the apartment building saying, "I think it's 'mission accomplished.' I was happy to just be a part of this. Why don't you come over to the house sometime after São Cristóvão and give me an update?" Goodbye was that "air kiss" business again and no touching.

105

5

NORTHEASTERNERS IN RIO – THE "SAGA" IN "CORDEL"

That week I went to the Casa de Rui and rummaged around in the "folheto" collection, plus found some notes on titles I brought from Lincoln. I came up with quite a list, many I was sure would not be at São Cristóvão. I made a xerox copy to give to Chico; I anticipated he would be excited, and I was not wrong. Maybe they would help with that sequel to "Pedro Pedreiro!"

Suspiros de um Sertanejo. João Martins de Atayde
   [A Backlander's Sighs]
A Secca do Ceará. Leandro Gomes de Barros
   [The Drought in Ceará]
Os Horrores e a Seca no Nordeste. Expedito Sebastião da Silva
   [The Horrors of the Drought in the Northeast]
O Sertanejo no Sul. Leandro Gomes de Barros
   [The Backlander in the South]
A Vida dos Seringueiros. Francisco Castro Brita.
   [The Life of the Rubber Gatherers]
Canção e Lamentos do "Soldado da Borracha" Raimundo Alves de Oliveira.
   [Song and Lament of the "Rubber Soldier"]
Os Martírios do Nortista Viajando para o Sul. Cícero Vieira da Silva (Mocó)
   [The Sufferings of the Northeasterner Traveling to the South]
O Choro dos Nortistas no Rio, Pau de Arara. Manoel Camilo dos Santos
   [The Laments of the Northeasterners in Rio, the "Hillbillies"]

O Nordestino no Rio. Manoel Ferreira Sobrinho. 1964
   [The Norteasterner in Rio]
O Agricultor Nordestino que Veio Trabalhar na Obra no Rio de Janeiro. Apolônio
Alves dos Santos.
   [The Northeastern Farmer Who Came to Work Construction in Rio de Janeiro]
Os Nordestinos no Rio, O Nordeste Abandonado. Apolônio Alves dos Santos.
   [The Northeasterners in Rio, the Northeast Abandoned]
Quanto sofre o Motorista e o Cobrador de Onibus. Cícero Vieira da Silva.
   [How the Bus Driver and Fare Collector Suffer]
O Trem da Madrugada. Azulão.
   [The Early Morning Commuter Train]
A Migração do Nordeste a São Paulo. João de Barros.
   [The Migration of the Northeast to São Paulo]

6

FRIEND HEITOR AND THE "PÉ SUJO"

It was an eventful week to say the least. On that day when I was looking for the migration "folhetos" at the Casa de Rui, and it was about closing time, I looked up from the reading desk and the familiar face of "old" friend Heitor Dias of the DOPS was in front of me, he strode in from the hallway.

"Miguel, I knew where to find you; I've been busy or would have made contact sooner, but this place is as good as any. First time I've been in here, but 'The Casa de Rui' is famous, and Rui is part of our history; those 'folhetos de cordel' you're reading I'm not so sure. It's funny they are here in one of the most renowned libraries of Brazil. How in the hell did that happen? Hey, you can tell me later. Even I know about Rui — a polyglot who could have taught the Queen of England English and a founder of the Hague, and also a candidate for President of Brazil."

"Oi Heitor, I figured we would meet again at some point, but I'm a bit taken aback to see a DOPS guy here with all the books. I bet you read up on the place just before you came. Just joking. What's up?"

"Miguel, I thought I'd take you up on that promise I made to you before you left last year. Why don't I give you a ride home, but we'll stop on the way at my favorite corner bar ["pé sujo"] in Copacabana and I'll buy you that drink I promised. Depending on you, we might even have time for dinner and a little fun later. Você topa? [Do we go?]"

I could see this was an invitation not meant to be turned down, so I said, "Topo. I like riding in your slick car anyway. Let me grab my briefcase and umbrella and we can take off."

Heitor had a driver who weaved through the early evening traffic jam from Botafogo through the tunnel and into that bright afternoon light of Copacabana. We didn't go far, just the other side of the old French luxury hotel, the Meridien, turned up a narrow cross street to a corner with a bar with lots of chairs and tables outside and most of them filled, the tables full of those big Brahma Choppe beer bottles in the Styrofoam holders. It was loud with much talking and joking. João (Heitor's driver) dropped us off saying he would check in in an hour.

Heitor said, "I'm officially off duty now, we can have a couple of drinks and get caught up. We know the story; Geroaldo up in Recife passed on the news of you and your time up there. Down here we've had people keeping an eye on you, no problem, just the usual 'drill;' you're in great standing with your diplomatic visa and so-called 'research.' What'll it be? Choppe or 'cachaça?'"

"I'm not into that straight rum, so how about the beer? Heitor, I could swear your coat is a little tighter since last year, you been a regular here?

He laughed, patted his belly and said, "Miguel, 'porra!' You've got to live a little and have some fun here in Rio even if you are a cop." Small plates of those good olives, slices of "salchicha" [sausage] and cheese appeared, the waiter giving Heitor a big smile; they seemed to be on a first name basis. Heitor sampled a bit of everything, took a swig of "choppe," lit a Marlboro (illegal by the way, still a big "moamba" [smuggling] item in 1970,) offered me one which I took and said, "Business before pleasure. Miguel, we've got you 'covered' at the Ferreira household. Sorry, by the way, Cristina seems to be 'off limits' now, her 'noivo' Otávio is a straight-shooter and is on our 'watch list.' Ole' Dad Ferreira is keeping it legit for now, so no complaints. But we are disturbed to see you are pursuing that project with Chico Buarque. I've got an almost verbatim record of your talk with Geroaldo in Recife (he was 'wired'), so no need to go into any of that. Suffice to say, Chico is on our 'close watch' list; he has to report to the downtown office every time he does a new song and our experts at the 'censura prévia' check out and approve or not any of the new songs. Porra, I've even become kind of a fan in all this business of keeping up with him. Tell me what your joint interest is and the project."

"Heitor, I've not sure it's any of your business, but the short version is I want to write up a special 'Letter' for the "New York Times" telling of what Chico and 'Cordel' have in common. So far, it's dealing with his music for 'Morte e Vida Severina,' his song 'Pedro Pedreiro,' and all the 'Cordel' stories on the drought and the migration to Rio and São Paulo. Nothing mysterious or particularly political, just telling the drama of it all. Hell, all my academic sources are in plain sight in that library you were just praising, the Rui Barbosa 'Cordel' collection. And Chico's stuff is known by almost anyone breathing in 'MPB' in Brazil."

"Miguel, for right now we'll just have to agree to disagree. All those MPB shitheads are on the Left, always have been. They may sing samba, but the message is trouble. You know about all that. No need to repeat it now, just that that is the main reason Chico got into hot water and still is. And I think I told you my view of all those damned 'nordestino' 'pau de araras' swarming over Rio like rats. It's a goddamned infestation. If they would just keep to themselves up in the North Zone and São Cristóvão on Sunday morning, that would be okay. Instead, they are hanging out in the Largo do Machado and even the plazas in Copacabana. Porra. You can spot 'em a mile away on the beach, those short, mixed blood chicks from the 'favelas' with their phony blond died hair. Some of my guys say they do have one redeeming quality – they know how to screw and are willing to do it for a free ride back to the North Zone and a few bucks. And the guys are all door men or watchmen and think they 'run' the city. I'd run all of them out of town."

"Heitor, have you ever read any of their stories in the 'Cordel?' I'll get you three or four, and you might change your tune. I think you might be surprised."

"Don't be in any big hurry."

7

THE BRAZILIAN PATRON SAINT AND OTHER MATTERS

Heitor went on, "Hey, enough of all this serious talk, how would you like to have a couple more beers and then see what the 'good life' really is in Rio. If you think that 19th century mansion on the beach in Flamengo is just an 'historic site' you've missed the boat. You want to meet some new people? I'll show you."

"Heitor, I have heard of that place, supposedly Rio's most glamorous house of prostitution. Things have changed some since last year; I've got a sweet lady waiting for me in D.C. and I don't need any scandal, hidden cameras or the clap. I can see going for a visit and maybe even writing up what I see for the 'Letters,' that might make for colorful and interesting reading. But I won't be going with the ladies. I'd have to go to confession after that."

"Porra, Miguel, you have my word we won't be taking any pictures or trying to frame you. Hell, if we took pictures, half the married men in Rio would be in divorce court, or maybe not. Women here expect this, and a lot of political and business deals get done there. As for confession, if you go to the right priest, he'll maybe tell you he's one of the good customers as well. We know you're not one of the rouge and lipstick 'veados,' [queers], already have proof of that from Geroaldo in Recife and your adventures at Boa Viagem and here from last year. So let's take a drive, I'll show you the place and introduce you to some friends."

For my friends who read "Letters," this is just a note on what most foreigners think they know about Brazil anyway, but it would make a good "short" in the movies. I can't help but think of Jorge Amado's tales of Vadinho and his friends in "Dona Flor e Seus Dois Maridos;" Amado's "castelos" in Bahia seemed like a helluva lot of fun when I read the novel – good times, dancing, drinking, lots of laughter, girls from Argentina, Paraguay and even Germany to pick from, not to speak of those gorgeous mulattas from Salvador. Every tourist in Rio has driven by the place in Rio; it's in the middle of Flamengo facing the beach, a relic of early 19th century architecture, a throwback to the glitter and glory of the Empire days. It has nothing on those mansions in Guatemala City and Mexico City I saw in 1962 in those student days but might come close to matching them.

Heitor's driver pulled off on one of those narrow side streets in Flamingo, drove a block or two, and dropped us off, Heitor telling him he would call when we were ready to be picked up. Heitor pushed the door buzzer, and soon it opened wide with a muted red light behind it (they must have had a camera trained on the entrance). A beautiful Brazilian girl the color of "café com leite" greeted us, gave Heitor a smack on the lips, quipping, "Mano,' are you getting too important to come and see us or has Graciela's across town offered you a better deal? And who is this 'filet mignon' [the slang term for a rich gringo most used by potential robbers ['assaltantes'] you brought with you?" (I could see the dollar bill signs in her eyes.)

"Miguel here is one of my assignments these days in keeping track of our long list of 'dubious persons' and their goings on here in Rio. He is a real 'arretado' – one helluva fine gringo – so I thought I would get him away from his books and the dust on the bookshelves at the Casa de Rui where he ostensibly is doing some research and brighten up his day. There's no book dust or book worms in here; the air is fine so let's have some fun. Miguel, tonight's on me, so if you want some of that foul-tasting imported Scotch, we've got it. What's your pleasure?"

"Mais um Choppe," [just another beer] will be okay. What's your friend's name? Maybe she can show me around the place."

The girl nudged up against me, whispered "Maria Aparecida," took my hand and glancing back at Heitor, said, "You know your way around and the girls will be glad to see you. Gisela has been in a funk since you disappeared two weeks ago, better go give her some attention. I'll take care of your friend. Jorge, our main bar man will bring your beer in a second." She walked me through a very large high-ceiling room, reminding me of what those main salons in the mansions in the old U.S. South might be, including a gorgeous rosewood winding staircase up to where all the business was to be done. All the furniture was non-tropical, over stuffed chaise lounges, divans, easy chairs. There was soft Bossa Nova music emanating from somewhere in the background. How can I say this? It was not really lavish but was not plain either. Several girls were sitting with men on the divans in various states of dress and demeanor, one with a leg over the man's leg, one bending low to lay her head in another's lap, he with a contented smile on his face, but most like in a regular upper-class bar-nightclub making small talk, having drinks and smokes.

"Maria Aparecida! That's a new one on me! The virgin patron saint of Brazil! Porra, Maria, how do you explain that?" By the way, as incredulous as it might seem, she had a tiny, gold cross on a chain around her neck, nestled nicely between a generous bust line.

"Miguel, if you know anything about Brazil, you know most of us are or at least used to be, Catholic. And when you are baptized here you get a saint's name. I was born on Maria Aparecida's feast day, so what do you expect? But if it makes you feel any better my friends here call me Lindalva, that means 'pretty dawn.' It's one of those old-fashioned romantic names of beautiful virgins from our 19th century Romantic Novels. Like 'Iracema' from ole' José de Alencar. How's that for irony! Here's your beer, drink up! And relax, Heitor already told me he's paying the bill!"

"Lindalva, you are one impressive chick. I don't mind telling you I've read a lot of Brazilian literature, including 'Iracema' and have run across 'Lindalva' in the folk ballads. I figure you must have done some studying in high school or college before you landed here! There's got to be a story."

"Miguelzinho, (now she was getting familiar), as a matter of fact, I actually have a degree in Letters from the USP, the University of São Paulo, but Literature teachers don't make a living here, particularly female teachers, and as you can see, I have other attributes than quoting from romantic novels." As she said this, she moved a little closer to me, and laid her arm in my lap. Uh oh, Gaherty's "stallion" was acting up in the mares' corral. I grasped her hand before any further damage could be done.

Thinking to myself, what in the hell now, asshole, you've got a job to do for "Letters," but the memory of Molly flashed through my mind. "Hey, Maria, you won't believe this bullshit, but I told Heitor I wanted to 'document'"what a really nice whore-house in Rio is like. So far, so good. But I'm a Catholic like you, St. Michael the Arch-Angel protecting us both from the snares of the devil and all that. And I've got a Catholic fiancée at home."

She convulsed with laughter, not an uneducated Maria Aparecida. "But what about 'Hail Holy Queen, Save Us from Our Sins and the Fires of Hell' and 'Angel of God, my Guardian Dear?' I think God will forgive you. After all, there's confession, and I have a good customer, Padre Ismael from St. Michael's by the way in Ipanema-Leblon, who can help you out if it really bothers you. I don't know what this 'documenting a whore house is,' but I can certainly dot the p's and q's. You need to get off that watered down 'choppe,' have a couple of our really decent 'caipirinhas,' we'll dance a bit. I know gringos can't dance samba, but we'll slow it down. If you've been to one of our 'gafieira' public dance halls, you'll catch on."

So we did that "slow dance" samba, cheek to cheek, breasts to chest, and with the expected consequences. Maria said, "Let's go upstairs, you need to see my 'office,' I'm kind of an 'upper echelon' host here." We walked to the back of the big salón, took an elevator up two floors, and were presented with a heavy carpeted hallway and one of the rooms to the side, a room with (ungodly!) a plastic plaque on the door, "Maria Aparecida, Boa Noite." Maria opened the door, said, "Miguelzinho, você está em casa." The walls were fillled with woodcut art, scenes from Bahia, Copacabana Beach, and a huge Cathedral Scene of Nossa Senhora da Aparecida. There was a big-screen TV, a cassete recorder with, can you believe it, Chico Buarque music playing (Heitor evidently had given her a preview of my tastes), a "frigo bar" to the side, and from the latter a bottle of champagne and glasses. She expertly and quickly I might add opened the latter, kissed me deeply on the lips, and said, "Let's see what you can learn about real Brazilian women for your 'documental.'"

Catholic scruples, a vague foggy plan to confess to Padre Ismael, and more importantly to Molly explaining how I had been seduced by Rio (ha!) came to mind. What followed was some of the hottest sex I could possibly have imagined. No apologies to Cristina Maria or to Molly, I was sweaty and limp when it was over. "Aparecida," as she really liked to be called, said (I'm not translating this; no harm done in Portuguese!), "O' Gringo! Você mesmo é um safadinho. Eu até experimentei um certo prazer no xuxu! Vou dizer ao Heitor que traga você de novo. Valeu a pena. Enchadão! E, nem vou cobrar! A 'propina' será uma boa conversa sobre a literatura brasileira!" Uma gargalhada tremenda saiu da boca da menina.

Minutes later, we took the elevator down, walked into the big salon and a smiling Heitor awaited us. "A successful research, professor? Hey, Aparecida, we got to hit the road, see you soon, that is me speaking for me, as for this 'arretado,' we'll see if he keeps his nose clean and out of trouble. I'll give you a call."

Back in Heitor's car, he patted me on the knee, said, "I'm taking you back to Dona Júlia's and hope you will write good things in the 'Letter.' Now, there's a favor you can do me, no pictures or any of that shit happened like I promised, but we need to know how you and Chico are getting along, the project and all that, and maybe anything he might tell you. Right?"

"Heitor, I appreciate the lack of photos, the great time with Aparecida; that won't be in the 'Letters' but the general description of a high-class Rio de Janeiro whorehouse will. But I have a problem with what I call this 'spying' on Chico business is. Merda, I've told you it's 'Morte e Vida Severina' and 'Pedro Pedreiro'and 'Cordel,' and that's it. What more can I say?"

"Está bem. For now. We're still buddies. And evidently you impressed Aparecida, that's no small deal with her experience. Porra, you must have picked up some tips from reading all that Jorge Amado sex shit. Miguel, be careful, these are dangerous times. Hey, I won't say you owe me one, but you owe me one. We'll drop you off at Dona Júlia's, but we'll be in touch. Hey, has your view of Rio been expanded, a little more uplifted shall we say?" He hee-hawed at the baudy humor. I had to admit, it was funny.

8

INCOGNITO TO THE SÃO CRISTÓVÃO FAIR

The following Sunday after a call checking in, I took a taxi to Chico's house in Laranjeiras and he was waiting for me at the door, dressed in "blue jeans" and a checkered shirt with one of those Irish-style "boné" caps, "In your honor Gaherty." Let's go! I've been looking forward to this."

We walked what seemed like forever to the "Jardim de Alah – Jacaré" bus stop, and just a few minutes later were on the bus with a rowdy Sunday morning crowd headed to the fair at São Cristóvão. Every time a new "pau de arara" got on, they would yell, "The gringo pays." Chico yelled back, "É, o dia de São Nunca" [a standard Brazilian joke when you complain no one pays his loans to you, "The Day of St. Never!"]! All laughed fortunately; it could have been different. The bus made its way through Copacabana, Botafogo and the freeway ["aterro"] downtown, swerving through sparse traffic and swerving some more as the "motorista" gunned the motor, racing a colleague on the "aterro." After lurching up Avenida Rio Branco to Avenida Getúlio Vargas, it headed west and then up the four lane to São Cristóvão. Chico commented, "This is a first for me! Porra, what a hoot!"

We pulled into the plaza, jumped off and he said, "Lead the way 'Gringo Arretado,' you're my 'cicerone' [guide] up here." We wandered through the "barracas" with food, clothes, tools, that smelly northeastern tobacco "fumo de rolo" and "cachaça" (Chico said, "We'll stop here on the way out") and then to the "Cordel" stands of Azulão, Apolônio Alves dos Santos and the old Antônio Oliveira, all old friends from my forays to the market. I introduced my new friend as "a buddy from São Paulo wanting to get to know "Cordel." We spied some of the titles I had listed on the "nordestinos" in the South, the ones about construction workers and the difficult life in Rio and Azulão's famous stories about "Zé Matuto no Rio" and "O Trem da Madrugada." Chico said, "This is a fucking gold mine; I'm not kidding, I'm going to do a sequel to 'Pedro Pedreiro', and I've got you to thank." Chico bought about twenty story-poems and tipped the poets. He said, "I've got to check out the music stands." I could barely hear him with all the noise. He said, "I had no idea there was so much music being created and produced here, all in the Luís Gonzaga 'forró' style. It puts MPB to shame!"

I said, "I've got a terrible headache from all this noise, not used to all the Brazilian 'movimento,' can we leave?" Chico said, "Just one more stop. We'll get something for the headache." We went back to the "cachaça" stand where he insisted I try about five "doses" [shots] all with different fruits. My head was reeling when he said, "Chega. Miguel, we've got to get you in training to drink like a real Brazilian! I don't think you are in shape for that bus ride, I'll get us a taxi."

I don't remember the ride home, the driver careening through the North Zone traffic and then through the tunnels back to Chico's house. He said, "Come on in, let's look over this great stuff I bought, and you can fill me in on the stuff you found at the Casa de Rui." The maid brought cafezinho and I downed two or three of the fiery hot, sugar loaded cups before I was revived. I had brought along the latest "Letter" reviewing our original interview and after he read it, he said, "Approved. Fine. No harm done here, and you've said it well. It won't hurt for the New York Times readers to read this stuff, porra, it might even sell come LPS. Go ahead with your research and just keep me up to date on progress. Hey, a change of topic. I've got another idea to show you more of Rio; I don't invite just anybody, but I need to know, are you a good walker and ready to see something different? I'm a notorious walker on some outings and places here in Rio I'm sure you haven't seen. You wanna tag along? One good turn (the Feira) deserves another. But I'm warning you, I walk fast, you'll sweat a lot especially if we get sunshine."

I could not believe my good fortune. Chico said, "I go early, just after sunrise. Wear some good sneakers, just walking shorts, a hat for the sun, and a light jacket, and I'll have water bottles. You've got a treat in store. I go every day, but during the week is best, fewer 'tourists' on the trail. How about next Wednesday? Come to the house and we'll have an adventure. Topa?"

"What can I say? You bet. Next week, Wednesday, and I'll call you and bring you the 'Cordel' northeastern migrant stories I xeroxed at the Casa." I hopped the Laranjeiras bus back to Posto 6 and Dona Júlia's house and Sunday dinner, but, no surprise, there was Heitor leaning against the fender of that black DOPS car. He was smiling, a good sign, smoking another Marlboro, waved for me to stop and launched into a one-sided conversation.

"Oi Miguel, how are you? Have you recovered from Aparecida? She's been asking about you. Evidently you made quite an impression. Next time your bill is on you, however. I'm just checking in. Looks like you and Chico survived the bus ride to São Cristóvão. How you put up with that noise, bad smell and 'nordestino' shit I'll never know. But no harm done. We've read your last 'Letter,' and all seems on the up and up, just that academic stuff you're sending to New York. Keep up the good work, and we'll be in touch by and by. What's next by the way?"

"Since you know it all anyway, I might as well tell you Chico is taking me on one of his hikes, I'm thinking up to the 'Floresta' [the "Floresta de Tijuca," the remains of the rain forest high above Rio], hopefully next Wednesday. I'm hoping to be able to keep up with him and maybe see some of Rio's wildlife, and I don't mean Aparecida's place. In the meantime, several 'Cordel' stories have come out and I'll be working on that all next week. They are about Garrastazu Médici's latest. Thanks again for the outing, no confession time yet but a lot of explaining to do back home. But that's another story. See you next time."

9

"LETTERS" – THE "BRAZILIAN ECONOMIC MIRACLE" – "FUTEBOL 1970"

I had time that week to catch up on "Letters" including the interaction with Chico, his music and the "Cordel" connection. We would talk later about that. But now, even though "Cordel" was indirectly saddled with the AI-5 "prior censorship," there were a few titles that came out which were useful for "Letters."

These months marked the beginning of the "Brazilian Economic Miracle" ["O Milagre Econômico Brasileiro"], the regime's "Macro-Economic Plan" to make Brazil one of the leading Third-World countries (striving to become First World) through huge economic investments in infra-structure, all to be based on loans from the IMF and World Bank. It was to be the basis for massive industrialization of Brazil. It was many faceted, and "Cordel" would report it all. It was the era of the rise of one rotund Delfim Neto, the economic chief and "brains" behind much of it in his role as an assistant, then, Minister of Finance. The Military would bake one huge "cake" of the Brazilian economy and everyone would get his "slice." Well, maybe. Not everyone. Once again, the rich with connections, anyone linked to the huge construction companies and the materials it required (ironically Ferreira my friend would get a few small contracts). There were many facets to the plan.

Dams, highways, bridges, telecommunications via satellite – were all part of the plan. For massive gains in manufacturing, including the national steel mills, auto manufacturing plants and a huge increase in the big machines for building roads, and also mechanizing the national agriculture, one needed power, and in Brazil, that meant hydro-electric power with all its huge rivers and their potential. So priority number one was the Itaipu Dam, eventually for a time to be the largest in the world. The concept went back to the mid-1960s when Brazil and Paraguay first began talks on its possibility (the river to be dammed was the "Alto Paraná" dividing Brazil and Paraguay and flowing then into Argentina). In 1970, during Garrastazu Médici's first year, a consortium of two major companies, one from the U.S., the second from Italy were awarded contracts for the viability of the dam. It would be huge, would fulfill the Brazilian dream for enough electricity and would make politicians (military and their cronies) rich with the contracts. And of course, there were the huge construction and concrete companies, all vying for contracts, i.e. bribes to politicians.

Just as important and in economic tandem would be the construction of roads and highways, but here is where it got interesting. Brazil always had a dream of westward expansion (many likened it to "Manifest Destiny" in the United States), so now was the time. With public relations companies churning out slogans it all began: "No One Can Hold This Country Back" ["Ninguém Segura Este País"] and "Brasil p'ra Frente" ["Onward Brazil"] and a sinister corollary, "Brasil – Ame- o ou Deixe -o" ["Brazil – Love It or Leave It"]. Delfim Neto was Minister of Finance during the exuberant economic growth years of the so-called "Miracle," the height being during Garrastazsu Médici's regime. Even at its start in 1970 the economy did boom, more than 10 per cent GNP.

The West of Brazil was largely undeveloped in 1970, a combination of savannah forest in the center and rain forest (the Amazon in the North, North Central and West). The military had a plan to build roads and open it all to economic exploration (and exploitation) and agriculture. There was a small diplomatic glitch: Chile, Peru, Ecuador, Colombia and Venezuela, Brazil's neighbors to the Southwest, West and North, did not applaud. The Armed Forces in Brazil, now in cahoots with the U.S. and enjoying its massive military aid, were every day growing and modernizing. To put it simply: If Brazil's "Marcha ao Oeste" ["March to the West"] reaches its logical conclusion, would it be expanded to "A March to the Sea?" It didn't happen, but the road did.

The Trans-Amazonic Highway would become a massive construction project beginning in 1970 in Garrastazu Médici's regime, but something else happened just months before it started in João Pessoa, Paraíba on Brazil's east coast - the World Cup in Mexico City. It was happening in May and June. When I showed Chico a "Cordel" story about it, he went nuts! I had learned he was a good Brazilian, that is, a life-long fan of the game, including his own "amateur league" team of buddies playing in his own tiny stadium of "Politeama."

At least a dozen titles reported on and opined about the Soccer World Cup and Brazil's victory that June, but the best might have been "O Brazil 1958-1962-1970 Tri-Campeão do Mundo." Written by a poet I had interviewed via the mail in 1966 for my dissertation, it put 1970 and the World Cup all into perspective in the "Cordel" world. José Soares known as the "poet-repórter" in Recife, the cradle of "Cordel" in the 1960s, wrote all kinds of story-poems about local and even national events. But one of his important sidelines was to show up at the local soccer matches and sell single-sheet broadsides with the "hot" results of the games; he became a fixture in Recife.

This story, with lousy metrics and rhyme (José was always in a hurry to "scoop" the major dailies for the games) was more important than most for a curious, but spectacular moment in Brazil. Not only did Brazil win the cup, the first to be tri-champion of the world, but its most famous "fan" was none other than President Garrastazu Médici, photographed in the stands in Guadalajara with a transistor radio to his ear and cheering for the national team. It was not all accidental – the Military had learned from Rome – bread and circuses might become "choppe" beer, carnival, the beach and "futebol."

Soares summarizes all the games leading up to the final and then the game itself. He knew this story-poem would make him a wad of cash (relative to a folk poet's world). He would dwell on the victory party days later in Rio Grande do Sul (Garrastazu's home state), contrasting that "fine" and "beautiful" football of Brazil with the rough and even dirty play in Europe, in this case, England (Chico would hoot and holler and almost collapse in laughter when I showed it to him).

In a play on words he told how Bulldog England and its rough game would be handled by Brazil's finesse with players like Jairzinho. Captain Carlos Alberto would not even respect Queen Elizabeth when he socked an English player trying to "club" him. And he praised the play of the now ole' master Pelé. The victory meant "carnival" in Brazil and José told how each player would celebrate in his home state but leaves the last to Everaldo for apparent reasons: it's beer, "Pitu," Port Wine and celebrations in Garrastazu Médici's home state.

10

HANGING OUT IN TIJUCA FOREST

Huge economic projects and change were in the air, but so far that summer no more than already reported. So I spent my time on the "Letters" account of Chico's songs and "Cordel" along with that promised walk up to the "Floresta de Tijuca." I arrived at his house in the back of Laranjeiras that Wednesday morning as promised, prepped with sneakers, walking shorts, a ball cap and t-shirt. It was early morning still a bit cool but promising a sunny day and tropical humidity. "Pronto? 'Bora." He took off like someone wanting to catch the last train out of Central do Brasil, walking swiftly and talking only when we stopped to rest (mainly at my request). We walked through the big iron gates of the Jardim Botânico, past the Emperor Palms and Orchid house, and along a sidewalk, then a sandy trail out the back. That was when we started to climb.

We would eventually get on the "Estrada da Vista Chinesa" ["The Chinese View Road"], but on the way there was a long and steep hike with several stops at my request and Chico's "mini-lecture" on Tijuca. The path, sometimes sandy gravel, sometimes road wound its way past heavy forest and occasional waterfalls to the top. On one rest stop Chico explained that this amazing forest was actually planted in the 19th century to overcome the erosion of sugar cane and coffee growing up on top and a threat to Rio's water supply. The replanting was done in a smart way, using and transplanting original trees and plants from what remained of Brazil's Atlantic Rain Forest. It worked and thrived.

We frequently ran into animals scurrying into the underbrush or heard them. Chico said he often sees possums, agouti (like a small capybara), lots of marmosets (saguí monkeys), an occasional sloth or armadillo and on rare occasions an ant eater. And you hear monkeys in the trees.

The other noise was the birds, much harder to see but Chico seemed to know their calls (he said he was going to write a song about them soon, mainly because they were gradually disappearing, he thought because of the pollution in Rio and the ever-growing population). We did see hummingbirds, one with a brilliant blue throat, another with brilliant purple, but the best was, and I even got to see it for a bit, was a small toucan of amazing colors. Chico said it was an "araracari-poca" ["saffron toucan"] yellow breast and a blue-red bill. There were lots of tiny birds that I couldn't begin to recognize but Chico said they were flycatchers, parakeets, tanagers or warblers all the time. I asked how he knew all this, and he shrugged his shoulders and said, "A good bird book, an encyclopedia and good eyes. Oh yeah, and maybe a walk up here once a week whenever I can."

After all this, as if the walk and nature were not enough, we arrived at the top of the "Estrada" and to the most spectacular view of Rio I had ever seen. It was incredible – the Statue of "Cristo Redentor" on Corcovado Mountain far off to the left, the Jardim Botânico in the center where we had started the hike, Sugar Loaf farther yet, but now in the center, the whole of the Rodrigo de Freitas Lake, Ipanema and Leblon and the ocean to the right and the Dois Irmãos Rocks to the far right. It was dazzling. Why they did a Chinese Pagoda on the spot I never found out.

Chico said, "Most people take taxis up here, but there are more and more hikers these days. I used to pretty much have it to myself during the week. But hey, 'gringo arretado,' what do you think?" After all we had seen on the way up, it was overwhelming. "What can I say? You delivered! I'll never forget all this. In Nebraska we've got Sand Hill Cranes along the Platte River, meadowlarks and some prairie song birds, but nothing like this. I guess we should plant some trees."

Just then, Chico noticed a chunky guy with a loose blue sport jacket and slacks on the other side of the "Vista" who was waving at us from a parked black sedan, using that Brazilian motion of palm of your hand down and waving your fingers. It couldn't be a mistake, it was "Come here." Chico did not hesitate, but laughed saying, "Hey, it's all cool. I know this guy. He's from the DOPS; they know I do this trail at least once a week and I guess they are looking for any 'funny business,' maybe meeting Communists or Ché Guevara or maybe I have a secret recording studio up here doing anti-government ditties. Ha ha! Porra! They generally have this guy or someone else up on top and another when I exit the Jardim Botânico on the way home."

"Oi Joaquim! De novo. Let me introduce a friend, Miguel Gaherty from the U.S.; he's a prof at the University of Nebraska, wherever that is, I think in the US backlands ['sertão,'] a writer for the 'New York Times' and doing reports for INR-WHA on Brazil. He's working with me on my songs related to 'nordestino' folk poetry, and I thought I'd show him something he'll never see in Nebraska. What's new my friend?"

"Nada de novo. Just the normal routine; no one's upset, and everything seems normal. Good to see you again, enjoy your walk. My boss Heitor already filled me in on this guy and some 'doings' of research with you. So be it. Hey, did you hear someone spotted a big cat ['onça'] up here a few days ago, so be careful."

"That's gotta' be bullshit Joaquim. The nearest ones are out in the Pantanal. Sounds like more Rio gossip to me. We'll be careful."

The walk down was of course much faster, and Chico seemed to be in a big hurry to get back home. He said he had a date at the recording studio on Monday and had to polish the two songs for the new 45 rpm and thinks this next song may get the DOPS' attention. Summer was moving along, my research was winding down, amid thoughts of returning to Nebraska and the books, and to Molly in D.C. I promised Chico I would get him a copy of the final draft of the paper on his songs and "Cordel" and also share any new items.

11

BAD NEWS AT THE FERREIRA'S

I was tying up loose ends reading "Cordel" at the Casa de Rui and needed to check in with Cristina Maria and the Ferreiras before heading home via my now annual "report" to Hansen of the "Times" in NYC and to see Molly in D.C. (I forgot to say I did send her letters during the trip and made one phone call.) I called, and Cristina said, "Miguel, something horrible has happened. I can't really talk about in on the phone, so can you come by this evening for a bit?" She seemed pretty shook on the phone; everything had seemed to be going so well earlier in the summer, so I was unprepared for what awaited.

When I rang the doorbell, a red-eyed Cristina answered, put her arms around me and was quietly sobbing, saying "It's Daddy." We went into the living room and were sitting on the divan, her mom Regina soon joined us. Cristina went on, "Last Thursday Daddy got a call from the downtown office of the DOPS, 'inviting' him to 'depor' ('explain yourself,' that's the way they operate) on some of his business practices with the concrete company, meaning his customers. You don't turn down their 'invitation.' Evidently it happened in the middle of the questioning. He had a heart attack. DOPS called us and we managed to get him into Santa Úrsula hospital. He's out of intensive care but had been ordered absolute rest, no work, at home." Regina just nodded her head, wiping her eyes with a tissue.

"My God, I'm so sorry. I feel pretty helpless. What can I do? I think this is important family time, so I'll make it short. Please give him my best; I'm sure with time he will be back to normal He has been so kind to me, in fact all of you, and made my time here in Brazil so rewarding. As of now I'm just preparing to go back home and don't really know when I'll be back again. Research goes well, including the project with Chico Buarque. I'll keep in touch via letter when I get back home. Once, again, I don't imagine there is anything I can do but let me know if there is."

I stood up, gave her Mom a hug and then Cristina Maria showed me to the door, gave me a big embrace and said, "I'm so upset now I can't really even think straight, but Miguel I'll write you in Nebraska with news and let you know how I, for that matter, all of us, are doing. Please remember our better times, I'll never forget them for sure. Maybe when things settle down, I'll be able to think about other things and appreciate your time this summer, the great moments with Chico." She did surprise me by a quick kiss on the lips as I went out the door.

12

PUBLIC RELATIONS IN THE OFFICE OF "PRIOR CENSORSHIP"

Departure was set for the following Wednesday, Varig to New York, the train down to D.C. to see Molly, TWA home to Omaha, and finally a bus to Lincoln. I figured I better make a last call to Chico and got quite a jolt on the phone.

"Oi, Miguel, I think I've got one last surprise for you in Rio. I don't know if you've heard but one of my new songs is making quite a stir. 'Censura Prévia' from downtown wants to talk to me about it. This stuff is 'old hat' by now; I'm used to it. I'll give them some bullshit and try to 'driblar a censura.' The surprise was one of the General's flunkies asked me to bring you along. They work hand in hand with the DOPS and the SNI (National Information Service, kind of like your FBI), and know of our meetings, project and outings. Sorry, ole buddy, but I think you and I have more than a friendship and research going as far as DOPS is concerned.

"I think since you're pretty familiar with my songs and have your New York and D.C. connections, they are thinking having you as a witness might generate good relations with the U.S. In fact, if all goes well, it might even be a way for them to get some favorable publicity in the U.S. Having you see they are just 'protecting the country and democracy' and the 'Great Brazilian Economic Miracle' they are bringing to Brazil. I warn you ahead of time, all is not quite what it seems. The guy in charge of it all, the General himself is in the room, and it's like a pleasant conversation, just asking a few questions for me to clarify the lyrics of the songs. Sometimes they say yes, sometimes they say no. They are not quite literary or poetic geniuses, so most of the time my lyrics get approved, but sometimes not, but for stupid reasons. In all honesty, it's a pretty dicey thing. On the one hand I've had a lot of success and popularity here in Brazil; on the other, they are paranoid about ANY opposition these days. It would be big news if they really screwed around with me. Anyway, I guess this is turning out to be a 'command performance' for both of us. I'll pick you up Monday at 1:00 and we'll head downtown, okay?"

So it went. The building and offices just off Avenida Rio Branco were innocuous enough, "Brazilian bureaucratic," stone on the outside with a central stairway up to the main floor, dark wood lined walls in the corridors, the waiting room and finally the large, well lit "office." It sure as hell wasn't like the somber, depressing, plain places I remembered from Heitor and the DOPS questioning a few months ago.

Chico introduced me and I think that's when the "spin" and the propaganda machine started revving up. Readers are familiar with some of the matters from me in prior "Letters," but you don't edit the General himself who said, "A pleasure to meet you Mr. Gaherty. We have word of your fine work in the 'Letters' to the 'New York Times' and your reporting of things Brazilian to the INR-WHA. I've read one or two of them myself. I would think you would be thrilled to meet Mr. Buarque de Hollanda, one of our great composers of popular music and samba. And he in fact ought to be in Rotary International for providing you, our guest, that spectacular tourism up to Tijuca Forest. And maybe you for escorting him to the Fair at São Cristóvão. I was apprised of it all, thank you.

"I've invited you here today to experience and perhaps gain some insight into what our 'Prior Censorship' Program ['Censura Prévia'] is and why we do it. (Sounded like a damned Rotary speech to me.) There has been a lot of misunderstanding and one or two uncomfortable incidents related to it. I would like your NYT readers to know <u>why</u> we initiated it. It is common knowledge that the only reason we are in governance is to save Brazil from the threat of international communism and specifically the threat of the expansion of the Cuban Revolution and its activities into Brazil, especially the Northeast. That is why we deposed the communist, leftist Brazilian president João Goulart back in 1964 and have since then brought Brazil to its senses, largely that is, and with some exceptions.

"The latest problem goes back one year ago. We experienced a really bad time in the middle of and late in 1969; kidnappings of foreign diplomats in Brazil increased by the leftists, largely for publicity and for leverage to free leftist prisoners we were holding, and with good reason, but the kidnappings generally backfired. The Brazilian public did not appreciate that our country would be known in the world as such a dangerous and unlawful place – diplomats in effect are 'out of bounds.' However, the violence grew with sporadic bank robberies and the like. We had no choice but to 'up the ante' and we did it with our mechanism of governance – the Institutional Act – in this case number 5. Among other things it established 'prior censorship' ['censura previa'] as a means to nip problems in the bud, that is, leftist criticism of the regime and our really ingenious plans to develop Brazil. I'm sure you are familiar with our motto of 'March to the West' and the opening of the Amazon Basin to development, the building of major hydroelectric projects for power for our industrialization and other major works of infrastructure.

"But back to the censorship; it mainly affects the press, national newspapers, magazines and TV, but because Brazilian Popular Music plays such an important role in the national psyche through its major appearance in the midia, and because some composers and musicians have unjustly and radically criticized the regime in their songs, we now require that all new musical compositions and recordings be reviewed <u>prior to</u> their release. That brings us to our relationship with Chico, and the meeting today.

"You must be familiar with the past few years when many musicians have gone into 'voluntary exile' rather than submit to our rules and regulations. Chico is one, with that one year's 'voluntary exile' in Italy. He was allowed to return, in part because of all that Brazil owes to his father, one of our major historians, and his uncle, the linguist with the definitive Brazilian Portuguese Dictionary, the famous "Aurelião." But he returns knowing the boundaries of any songs and lyrics concerning the regime. So now and again we meet here in this office to review his latest compositions. And that's what brings us together today. Mr. Gaherty you have full permission to write your report for 'Letters,' unless I say, 'off the record.'"

Not knowing what in the hell to say, but thinking, "Don't screw this up, asshole," I said to the General, "This is certainly a new experience for me since I've heard so much about the 'prior censorship,' but I can assure you I will write my 'Letter' with utmost care, reflecting the meeting today."

Chico had been silent through all this, quite a change of demeanor for him, but I assumed he knew the "drill" and was not about to make light with the General or his task. He said, "General, I'm pretty sure I know why I've been called for this visit. Could you enlighten me?"

"Chico, it has to do with one of your latest compositions and the amazing press and popularity it is experiencing all over Brazil right now. Some have gone so far to say that it has become the 'anthem" of national protest, a rather significant turn of events would you say? I'm of course talking about 'Apesar de Você' ['In Spite of You']. I realize it passed 'first review' of the censorship but cannot imagine why.

"To put it in a nutshell, you present a pretty dismal picture: people not able to talk openly, but just having to follow orders, mumbling in the streets to themselves, heads down. And the 'you' who invented it all, invented sin but no forgiveness. And in spite of 'you' there will be a better day and great euphoria. 'And I'm' going to get even, have my revenge and where will you hide? It will be a bitter day for you, and I'll die laughing.'

"Chico, I'll go straight to the matter. There are many, and my closest advisors among them, that say the 'you' in this song refers to our President Garrastazu Médici and to the regime and current status of the country. If that's so, and you know our recent actions regarding the distribution of the song, we cannot possibly allow further sales of the recording in any form nor performance, recorded or live, on the national media. And furthermore, we've been rather subdued in our dealings with you; that is subject to change at any moment."

It was finally Chico's turn.

"General, if you'll pardon me (no pun intended), I wrote that song in a fit after Marieta my wife and I had a huge fight a few weeks ago. What it's really about is a very bossy woman. I don't know how things are with you and your wife, and I certainly don't dare to presume, but have you ever had a 'knock down and drag out?' I'm thinking most married people have. If that's the case, and you look at these lyrics carefully, you'll see exactly what I mean. I was really pissed off ['puto da vida']. Now, I'm not saying for the record that the woman in the song is Marieta, God help me (he laughs) and please don't read anything into it. But I will say that was why I was so damned mad. Hey, it's a song; it's poetry. And there's such a thing as poetic license. It's just all about a bossy woman."

The general smiled, nodded his head in agreement and patted Chico on the shoulder, and looked over at me, "Okay, the prosecution rests, notwithstanding our recent confiscation of the disks in the stores. But just for now. Mike, I think you should edit your story, no mention of Marieta for Chico's sake. You can say that we in this office are satisfied with the explanation and despite what Chico says, we do know poetry when we see it. And I have heard of poetic license.

"Mike, just an aside, I had a Brazilian Poetry class with your old mentor Colonel Manuel Cavalcanti Proença back in the very early 60s at the War College (he taught literature to the officers), and we talked about a lot of this stuff. I'm not 100 per cent convinced the song can't have another 'reading' (Manuel taught us that too), but like I say, for now all is well. Chico, that's all for today, but we will definitely be in touch.

And Mike, I wish you a great trip home and will be looking forward to reading the 'Letter,' as advised by the way. Okay?"

We shook hands, and Chico and I walked down the steps out on the street, he saying, "Porra. I've got to have a drink, and not watered-down beer. Let's take a taxi home and I'll give you my 'take' on all this. You can tell me what you think of Brazil and our glorious leaders after that."

When we got into the house Chico poured himself a shot of "cachaça" and got me a beer, sat down on the divan and suddenly began to laugh. It took a while for him to stop. "Miguel, driblei a censura de novo" ['I fooled the censors again']. All I have to do is talk to Marieta and make sure she's in on the joke. It's like all my songs; I leave it up to the person who hears it to decide for himself. In this case and I don't think you knew, when I did the song and submitted it to Censorship before the recording session two weeks ago, I was sure it would not pass, but 'porra,' it did. Just last week over 100,000 copies were sold. DOPS, seeing that, had a change of mind and tune and went to the record stores, confiscated any records left (the General mentioned that in passing), closed the recording studio in Alto da Boa Vista in Rio and called me in to 'depor' ['testifify']. You know the rest of the story; you were there. But thousands of Brazilians who have already bought or heard 'Apesar de Você' may have already formed an opinion; that business of the anthem against the dictatorshit, or should I say, dictatorship, is ringing true. So, how about all this?"

"Chico, I would say you are fortunate to not be in one of those dark cells for dissidents. The only thing I can figure, is, like the General said, your family and your own past visibility in Brazil must have allowed the leeway. But I sure as hell would be careful from now on. If it's okay with you, I'll write up the interview with the General, make sure it has a 'cleansing,' get a copy of the 'Letter' to you and the General. But all that will happen a few days after I'm out of here and back in Nebraska. And I'll be writing up the research article this coming winter and will send you a copy before I submit it for publication. There's no doubt a major publisher well be interested, thanks to you, not me. And Chico, I just want to say, this has all been great, far more than I could have dreamed of. Not just the research but the friendship. I don't know exactly when I'll be back in Brazil, but I hope I can give you a call and we can renew our friendship."

"Miguel, com certeza! And when we're back together I'll show you the lyrics for a sequel for 'Pedro Pedreiro,' which I can guarantee will be a hit. And thanks to you. The only thing I didn't get you to is one of my team's 'futebol'matches, but we'll work on that next time. Think of us all here in Brazil and even a prayer or two would not hurt. I think there are dark days ahead."

With those words echoing in my mind I packed my bags, got all the new research together, made a last good-bye call to Cristina Maria to check on her father, and her by the way, and began that process of "mental re-entry" to reality back home. Not wanting to risk delays, I splurged on a "radio taxi" to the Galeão for the international flight on Varig to New York. Hansen had asked for our "decompression" talk and offered to put me up for a night in the city, another meal and plans for "Letters." And then, there was Molly.

13

"DÉJÀ VU" AT THE
AIRPORT EXCEPT …

Not unexpectedly while checking in early for the Varig flight, old friend Heitor Dias came up to me in the line, a smile on his face, and said, "We've got to say goodbye once again, but before that there is someone who wants to meet you." "Déjà vu all over again" as Yogi Berra would say. Didn't this happen when I left in 1969? Heitor commented that uptight gringos always checked in early, so there was plenty of time. We ended up in the same DOPS room as last time. There was a gentleman in a dark business suit, grey tie and a very neat and crisp demeanor, a lot snappier than Heitor's usual. He was middle aged, probably in his late 1940s, tall for a Brazilian, and with a physique of an athlete.

Heitor said, "Miguel I want you to meet Colonel Oriosvaldo Ramos. He is the person in charge of the main desk of our SNI in Rio, that's the 'Serviço Nacional de Informação,' kind of like your FBI. We at DOPS work closely with them."

Colonel Ramos shook my hand, asked me to sit down on one of those hard, uncomfortable Brazilian office chairs, and introduced himself, "Senhor Gaherty, I'm sorry to take your time, but I think our meeting will take no longer than an hour and you'll have ample time to catch your flight. In fact, if we need to, we can nudge Varig to delay for ten minutes or so. Perhaps a bit of explanation is in order. The SNI is basically an intelligence gathering service, a "bank" as it were of all national surveillance data. While Heitor here and our friends in the DOPS are the on-the-ground police who keep track of politics and political movement in Brazil and lately of I A – 5 work with the Censorship people, we at SNI have a larger mission. We are the backbone of anti-communist action in Brazil and work closely with the CIE, "Serviço de Informação do Exército," [the Army Information Service]. They are the main entity fighting terrorism in Brazil, the kidnappings, bank robberies, and I daresay have been very successful as of late in their mission. And that brings me to you.

"As a gatherer of information, you yourself for your 'Letters' to the 'New York Times' and providing similar information to your own State Department via the INR-WHA will understand that we naturally have kept a file on your activities and findings here the last two years. In that file we have a list of all your contacts in Brazil, including the legitimate research and reporting you do, but also contacts with the Left, or at least sympathizers of the Left. That of course includes from way back your relationship with Colonel Cavalcanti Proença for your dissertation; you know he was asked to 'retire' in 1964 from active duty in the army but allowed to teach literature at the War College. But there are others, including Ariano Suassuna in Recife and your relationship with the Ferreira family and of course now Chico Buarque de Hollanda. All good and well. Your recent attendance at Chico's interview with General Goeldi of the Prior Censorhip Board has informed you of some of our government's activities and good intentions to preserve Democracy and peace in Brazil. What is new is a bit of information we just obtained through, shall we say an interview, with a leftist activist in Rio just last week.

"It may be a surprise to you, and it was mildly to us, one of the few remaining splinter groups of the Left, the ARB ("Ação Revolucionária Brasileira") cell in Rio, had plans to kidnap you, hold you for ransom from the 'Times' and INR-WHA. You are a very very lucky person Mr. Gaherty. The event was to take place on your way to the airport this morning. That radio-taxi you hired to pick you up in front of your boarding house was monitored by us. The result was two unmarked SNI cars in effect 'escorting' the taxi to the Galeão. ARB must have been suspicious of our little 'convoy,' because no attempt was made. I might add that both of our vehicles had a total of four highly armed anti-terrorist agents who would have made very quick work of any attempt to run your taxi off the road. So here you are, safe and sound, and now a bit wiser to the dangers you face in Brazil."

I was shaken and asked for a glass of water and a "melhoral," Brazilian aspirin. "Sir, how can I say it? I am grateful for all you have done. I would think I am surely 'small potatoes' (as we say in Nebraska) for such people. I will certainly inform Mr. Hansen of the Times and Mr. Iverson of the INR of your good work in protecting a U.S. citizen, researcher and journalist in your country."

Colonel Ramos said, "That, Mr. Gaherty, is the very next and perhaps last thing I wanted to talk to you about. We do in fact have a relationship, or understanding if you will, with your INR-WHA. It basically involves an exchange of information with the purpose of avoiding any embarrassing scandals or even libel against our government as a result of actions we might take to fulfill our own mission here in Brazil. Even though your case is, and I hope I don't offend you, a 'minor' one, Brazil does not need the publicity of one more kidnapping or even attempted kidnapping of a foreign representative in our country. So, this meeting and that event never happened, correct? And one more thing, we presume your role as researcher, journalist and liaison with INR-WHA will continue in the future, but we have a small favor. Should you return to Brazil in that capacity, or any other for that matter, we will want to be informed and in fact will be instrumental in approving or not your visa. It really does not change anything from what you already have or have not done but is just a precautionary action for all concerned so that in effect we can 'be on the same page.' I advise you to edit your 'Letters' carefully. We are not Nazis or Fascists here and can permit your thought and speculation as to our government and its actions, after all, we are trying to improve free speech, but in a measured way. But should we see in your 'Letters' unjust criticism that 'stains' our image, that would be the end of your time in Brazil, and I know that in the future you plan to teach Portuguese, our culture and history and publish your findings even here. So good luck and stay in touch."

"Thank you, sir. Back home we value free speech above all, a keystone to our democracy. And free speech is a requisite for 'Letters.' I will not want to feel 'hog tied' as we say in Nebraska, but I assure you that I will write with discretion as a journalist and researcher. You will be informed when I next come to Brazil."

We all shook hands, and Heitor escorted me back to the check-in line. He patted me on the shoulder, smiled and laughed and said, "Miguel, on a lighter note, maybe we can get back to the 'pé sujo' and to my 'office' to see Aparecida again. But seriously, you just dodged a bullet. Be careful. I'll miss you."

The hours rolled by and as I waited for the flight to New York, I did the usual diary notes, reviewed what I had planned for the next "Letter" to the "Times" and was beginning to think what I would say to Hansen, and later to Molly in D.C. Suddenly, I broke out in a cold sweat, "Holy Mary, it is just dawning on me what could have happened to me this morning on the way to the airport. I think I've been in shock. I remember the details of the Elbrick kidnapping in 1969, how he was roughed up, reacted and suffered physical and mental consequences he never recovered from. Maybe it's time for me to get back to church and mass and maybe even confession. Brazil took me away from all that, but Molly for sure won't mind if I'm back in the fold." I spent the rest of the time in the waiting room and the first couple of hours on the flight trying to sift through the fuzzy cloud of all that had happened the last few months.

After the evening meal I asked the stewardess for two of those little bottles of scotch, took two "melhoral" and went into a drowsy dream-sleep for the next eight hours. I awoke to the smell of good Brazilian demitasse coffee, the sun coming up in the East and the announcement that we were forty minutes from JFK. The old feeling had come back: I felt safe, was beginning to relax and was glad I was an American.

14

ALL'S WELL THAT ENDS WELL

Hansen had a man meet me at the exit from customs, a "Gaherty" sign in his hand, shook my hand, volunteered to carry my bags to a taxi and said, "If you don't mind, Mr. Hansen said he would prefer you meet in his office at the 'Times.' Is that all right?" What could I say, "Of course, I'm looking forward to it." The skyline of Manhattan in the distance across the East River, the fast run through the tunnel, and suddenly we were surrounded by the skyscrapers of New York. Located at 8th ave and between 40th and 41st street near the Port Authority Building the "Times" headquarters indeed is one of the true glass and steel tall buildings of New York. The reader may recall all my previous meetings were at delicatessans and the like, so this was a thrill and also a bit intimidating. I felt like I was in New York and not only that, but in the center of a thriving city – the Times Tower! Hansen's office in the international section on the 20th floor was I guess what he deserved and merited – a corner office looking to the skyline with the Empire State Building in the distance.

He welcomed me, tweed jacket and all, briar pipe on the desk, "Mike, Hansen just wired me of your little morning episode yesterday. My God am I happy you are all right. Let's break protocol a bit; I've got a bottle of some fine, strong stuff here somewhere. Do you want a snort? I think it's Glenlivit?" I hadn't had scotch all summer, but it really didn't matter. "Fine, Mr. Hansen. I'm still exhausted even though I did sleep a fair amount on the 8-hour flight from Rio."

"Mike, I think you can call me James by now, after all we are indeed colleagues in the news business. Give me your 'take' on the latest developments and then I'll have some ideas how we can proceed."

"Fine, James it is. I think all in all things went well in Brazil, about as planned with just a couple of glitches. The fact the SNI entered the scene at the airport and what could have happened has me shaking in my boots. On the other hand, it does not seem to me to really change anything, after all, whether it is DOPS or SNI, we're still dealing with Brazilian surveillance, in this case of me and my contacts. We know they are reading my 'Letters' and keeping track of basically all my contacts in Brazil. I don't much like the latter but can live with it. I am uncomfortable, thinking in the back of my mind, that I can't write anything, as SNI said, to 'stain' their reputation. You know all too well that they have put a 'spin' on their 'holy mission' to justify not only the revolution itself, but any subsequent nasty activities, and there are many. I think I or someone said, 'To save Brazil the made it one big military compound.' More important to me right now is your opinion of this year's 'Letters,' all these recent developments and where do we go from here."

"Mike, it's basically carrying out plans we made a year ago. This year's 'Letters' in my opinion were great, albeit changed some in tone. You still filled us in on happenings in Brazil, your research, but with those added tidbits on the sex life of the Brazilian male, or should I say, the red blooded American in Brazil, (handled with great discretion I thought in the 'Letter'), your dealings with Ariano Suassuna in Recife, the Ferreira family, and with Chico Buarque in Rio. Folklore at São Cristóvão and a bit of nature at Tijuca Forest added a nice note. The latter with Chico by the way was and will continue to be a big hit with our readers. And the fact he appoves of your article on songs and 'Cordel' plus the fact that the agent in the censorship bureau <u>asked</u> for your presence and report is huge. That my friend in our world used to be called a 'scoop.' It's our first witnessed account of the censorhip going on today by the regime. I would proceed 'with discretion' in regard to Chico; we don't want him in any hotter water than he already is. But your initial account of his songs and 'Cordel' are great; I await the final 'Letter' soon to come as to that. I'm sorry you and Cristina Maria did not work out but think that may for the best for all concerned.

"Mike, after consutation with my colleages here in the International Section, we had thought of offering you a full-time job as a reporter for us in Brazil; you are that valuable. You would get travel, living expenses and a decent but not great salary. But I'm not sure how that would be that that much different from marrying Cristina and working for her Dad in the concrete business in Brazil. You would still be living there full-time. Did I surmise correctly?"

I thought for a moment, but it did not take too long for an answer. "James, you are right. I love Brazil, love my research and especially now with the new developments with Chico Buarque, but hey, I'm still a professor at heart and am doing what I do best being in the classroom and doing some research along the line. And I don't know how

I could live in Brazil year-round, and certainly without Cristina or someone like her. I still do have that commitment to Molly here at home, although I'm not sure if 1970 in Brazil changed any of that. You know, she reads all the 'Letters' in the paper as well."

"Okay, that is about what I had expected. I think we have enough material for a book with 'Letters' from your last two stays in Brazil. They will need a rather large amount of rewriting and editing, particularly in lieu of the fact you are dealing with more sensitive persons and situations. And no small matter, I'd like you to think about a different title. Back to the sensitive: we have to be careful to not bring harm, physical or otherwise, to those you deal with, and especially to Iverson and others in the INR-WHA who have to deal with the quirks of Brazil on a day to day basis. Here's what I think: tie up all your loose ends in a final 'Letter,' maybe to me in a month, and then we will pursue the matter of the book. We'll use the same publisher; they generally don't turn down my recommendations.

"I've got a lot on my desk today, Mike, so if you don't mind, we'll close this conversation and take up subsequent matters by phone when you are back in Nebraska. I assume you may want to take the Amtrak down to D.C. for that 'other' matter, right? You can catch it early in the p.m. and see your sweetie tonight. I'll have someone call for a taxi over to Penn Station. It's close and will just take a few minutes."

15

IT WAS MEANT TO BE

I borrowed a desk phone in the office next door and called Molly at home. Luckily, she was still there, just in from an a.m. workout at the gym. I think we were mutually happy to hear each other's voice, but it was business over the phone. She would meet me at Union Station in D.C., and it would be just a short taxi to our old watering hole at the "Dubliner." Amtrak was due in at 4:30 and no weather that day. So I said, "I've missed you Molly. We've got a lot to catch up on." Her answer was a bit short, for her, "Mutual. Love you. See you in a few hours."

Auburn hair, green eyes, full figure beneath blouse and an attention getting short skirt showing off those great legs, Molly met me right out from the exit from the train. There was a huge hug, a deep kiss, and some tears of happiness and I daresay, relief, from both of us. We grabbed my bag and carry on, hailed a cab and did the short jaunt to the Dubliner, already starting to fill up with all those D.C. bureaucrats and maybe a few bigwigs as well. One of the booths in the back was free. We sat beside each other, piling all the stuff in the other seat, ordered a couple of Harps and began to renew the relationship.

Molly started, "Mike, I am so glad you are home safe once again. When I read that letter of you and Chico in the Censorship office, it honestly scared the crap out of me. I want to know all about it, but first there is one small complaint - just how many letters did you send me from Brazil? They seemed few and far between to me. We've got far more to talk about than Brazil, but let's save that for home and our real "reunion" tonight. I've saved a bottle of champagne or two and I'm sure we'll be up late."

"Molly, you know the hassle to even mail a letter in Brazil; I even wrote about it in one of the early 'Letters.' But I'm sorry I didn't write more, I think I mailed five letters in all. And we did have that one phone call from Rio. You know my policy, 'No news is good news.' When you get a phone call from me, it might not be a good thing. But I can't wait until tonight. Are we still "on" for December and the wedding? I'll just tell you, as of now there are no return trips planned for Brazil. And I told you the truth in that phone call from Rio – Cristina Maria is well into 'another' life with Otávio and her own wedding set for next summer. You are the only lady in my life."

Molly broke into tears and I wasn't sure why. "Damn, Molly, what's wrong? Is there something I don't know.? Something I did? Has something happened?"

She dried her eyes with a tissue from the purse, looked into my eyes, kissed me through the tears and said, "I am so relieved. Do you have any idea what you have put me through? Let's talk about it at home, I just can't handle the emotion of it all here in a damned booth in a bar. Let's have another beer, something to eat, and then a taxi home. Maybe you can just fill me in on those last days in Rio after the Censor and Chico. I can handle that."

"Molly, there's not too much to add, just one item. I expected the DOPS to check me out in the airport, probably old friend now Heitor of the Rio section, but when they called me from the Varig line to the DOPS office, there was a surprise. I got to meet Colonel Ramos of the SNI, kind of like our FBI. There was no hassle, but he just was informing me that I have a file in the national information bank. The surprise was, are you ready, there was a leftist plan of a splinter group in Rio to kidnap me that morning on the way to the airport. SNI learned of it via what I imagine was a torture session, contacted the DOPS, and in effect arranged (unknown to me) an armed escort to the airport. (Molly gasped at this news.) As you can see, I'm safe and sound and no worse for wear, but I guess I have not allowed myself to think of what <u>might</u> have happened. I'm certainly small potatoes for ransom, but I think it was the link to the "Times" that figured in their plan. Anyway, Colonel Ramos cautioned me on my next trip, should there be one, and said he wanted prior arrival plans, an itinerary and the like, all I surmise to protect me. But we don't have to worry about that; there are no trips planned for Brazil for a while."

Molly gulped down her drink and said, "That's enough on my plate for now. Let's get out of here." We lugged all my luggage and stuff to a cab and went directly to her apartment near Dupont Circle. I had scarcely dropped my bags when I was enveloped in her huge hug and kisses. We just both stood there a while, both of us I guess needing that closeness. Molly said, "There's a bottle or two of champagne in the frig; let's open one and change the subject to happier things. Just know, I don't much like all these things you do in Brazil and just wish you could do your research in the library back at Lincoln."

I said, "Molly, so do I for right now and that's the plan for this fall and winter. But I've a surprise for you." I pulled a small packet wrapped in string out of my briefcase, untied it and poured the contents on the small dining nook table. There was a good pile of Brazilian semi-precious stones – amethists, tourmalines, topaz and aquamarines, and in all sizes. I said, "All for you Molly; take your pick. I'm hoping we can save a half dozen for your Mom and my Mom and sister Caitlin."

Molly was and is not a social climber and never had been interested in anything ostentatious, but her eyes grew big seeing all the stones. "Where in the world did you get these? I know you had a budget but not for this kind of stuff." I said, "It was a friend in Rio whose Mom likes jewelry and has a wholesaler from Minas Gerais come to the house a time or two per year. What you see is what she convinced him to offer me with a big discount." Molly thought for a minute, and said, "You know that gorgeous tourmaline (it was green and looked a bit like an emerald, that is, if you did not particularly know your stones), or that baby blue aquamarine, either one would make a terrific engagement ring. We can get a gold setting and maybe put a small diamond to each side. What do you think?" "Fine with me, I just wanted to please you." (A couple of weeks would pass, and Molly in a call said the ring was ready and although inexpensive by most standards, I discovered that jewelers still make their bucks; the cost of the "setting" was a lot more than what the stone cost.)

"So, bring me up to speed on the wedding. Molly I have to know if you still feel the same. I do, so the sooner the better."

"Mike, I've given it a lot of thought and talked to Mom about it. She said anytime is fine, but I think we should not be hasty. You've just been in Brazil, far from me, and I know there are still emotions going on about that. I mean Cristina, even though you've told me her situation and plans. I'm thinking, let's get through the academic year, I'll come out to Lincoln once or twice, you can come here, and if things go well, we can have a June wedding. I'm supposing and counting on you not going back to Brazil next summer. If we have two or three months' notice, let's say by mid-March, we can still do that June wedding. You get off easy; it's always the bride and her mother who do most of the work. I've got some ideas, but since you went to Georgetown maybe we can rent the chapel there. It will cost an arm and a leg, but now with you with that reputation for 'Letters' from the 'Times' and your upcoming book, I think the Jesuits would be glad to spare it for one day."

"Molly, as far as I'm concerned, we don't have to wait, but here's an idea: settle the chapel date now, let's see how the coming months go, and we can always cancel. But I don't need a June wedding either; how about semester break next year? Uh oh, I forgot about winter weather, but Georgetown is no picnic in June either. We can talk about all that more before I head out to Dulles for the flight home the day after tomorrow. Let's drink this champagne and get to know each other again."

Molly filled the wine glasses, we moved to the divan, and after opening the second bottle both of us caught fire for that old flame. I'll not go into details, but it was fun and convinced me I had not made the wrong decision about this girl. And I think she of me. It was a long night, lots of lovemaking, conversation and not much sleep, but the next day was beautiful, a few clouds, and Molly's coffee and toast to wake us up.

She said after a bit, "I've been thinking, and last night confirmed it. I don't think I can wait a full year and a half. If we both love each other, and our minds are made up, why wait? June has got to be it. You can go on back to Lincoln, we'll talk on the phone every day, and I'll get on with the planning. Just show up here in early June (oh you'll have to stay with one of your Georgetown buddies' apartments,) and we'll just do it!"

"Molly, sounds great to me. I do have to tell you I have a huge amount of work to catch up on, including writing the last "Letter," getting ready for classes in two weeks and mainly writing up the Brazil research for a couple of articles or maybe even a monograph. We can see each other at Thanksgiving, Christmas or better yet, combine Christmas with my semester break. Maybe you can get some extra time off from the gallery and we'll do a holiday trip to New York and maybe see snow in New England. How about a big date today: Let's go to the Mall; you know I love the Air and Space Museum and you love the Art Gallery and then we'll have a nice dinner out, you pick it."

"Fine, Mike, you and I always have a great time, let's go. We can take the metro and be on the Mall in a couple of hours."

"If I can keep my hands off you, and I don't guarantee it, we'll come back here tonight for further 'consultation.' You have some more champagne? Put it in the frig and I promise you an exciting evening."

And so it went, the Smithsonian Mall, a couple of museums, dinner at an Italian place down from Capitol Hill, back to Molly's apartment, another night of lovemaking, and me up early the next a.m., the metro to Dulles and the flight to Omaha and bus to Lincoln. Molly would put things in gear for a wedding in June, but there was a lot up in the air for her to find out and let me know in Lincoln. We said our goodbyes at the apartment, a bit of a sad moment, but both of us thinking of the future.

16

"THE DRILL" IN LINCOLN

Back in Lincoln it was the usual "drill," unpacking at the apartment, getting cleaned up and presentable for my "check in" interview with ole' Doc Hillardson, still my boss at the Modern Languages Department. He is a nice human being, a fine man, treating me yet, even though untenured, as an equal colleague. Over a coffee in his office, he said, "Mike, what's up? I've been following your 'Letters' to the 'Times,' so congratulations are once again in order. But tell me in a nutshell where you're at with things for us here at U of N."

"Professor Hillardson, it all went well, with a couple of glitches. In so far as you, the department and my work here, I can report that the book in Pernambuco is still in the works. I saw the list of publications due to come out there while at the Library of Congress Office in Rio, so it's legit, but they take forever. The first article at the National Folklore Institute is out and a second is actually at press in the Institute Review. But I'm most excited about the 'Letters' going well, a promise for a second book with the 'Times' in New York putting 1969 and 1970 together. The best thing about all this is that Volume II will have all the research and time with Chico Buarque de Hollanda, and it does not get any better than that. I was 'right on' in my guess of the close link between some of my work and his songs and hit the jackpot when he was so eager to work with me. In fact, it's on-going; I expect to be in touch with Chico soon in my work. If all this comes to fruition, I'll have three books, one in Brazil, two in New York, articles in refereed journals, so I'm assuming that puts me in good stead for tenure here. Oh, and on a personal note, I'm marrying my sweetheart from College Days in Washington D.C. next June, so things are really going well."

"Mike, I could not be more pleased; you'll be up for tenure in two more years and are in fact one of our 'young stars' in the Department. I know you are aware of

Professor Miller's opposition to your line of research, but he is just one vote on the committee. I say full speed ahead! Just keep doing what you're doing now. The students really seem to like you although they say you can be a hard-ass prof some days; you might work on that. Remember you're not at a Jesuit school any more! Just keep me posted on developments as they happen."

So, notwithstanding occasional frosty encounters with Miller, everyone else welcomed me back that Fall with open arms, and all were most genuinely pleased by the upcoming marriage. I settled in with a basic Portuguese language class, a Brazilian Literature class and a survey of Spanish Literature just to keep in touch. All my spare time was spent on sending the final "Letter" to Hansen, polishing all the "Letters" from 1969 and 1970 for the new "Times" book, and doing a lot of research on the "Cordel" story-poems and relating them to Chico Buarque's declarations from the summer. I enjoyed it all except for the bad news from Brazil.

EPILOGUE

"Cordel" in late 1970 was mainly silent other than reporting Garrastazu Médici's inauguration of the Transamazonic Highway. The axiom by one of the poets, "Politics is a dangerous plate in Brazil today," held true. It was not a time to be criticizing the government. Praise on the other hand, was welcome. The whole story of the highway was involved, but you had to give some credit to the President, perhaps because it all had started with his trip to a drought-stricken Northeast. He saw that nothing could be done for the drought, and for sure nothing could be done for the poor farmers badly in need of land reform which would have helped in the interior (land reform was a red line – it smacked of Cuba, Fidel, Ché and Communism and had helped torpedo Goulart's regime in 1964). But a "pulga na orelha" ["cunning idea"] came to the President from his economic "assessores" [advisors] – why not open up the Amazon to homesteading, offer land to the peasants and get some of them out of the Northeast? This idea of course was hinged on transportation, infra-structure and getting people and products in and out of the vast Amazon area. The answer was Garrastazu Médici and cohorts' brainstorm – the Transamazonic Highway from the Atlantic to the border of Peru, beginning by no accident in impoverished Paraíba State and its capital, João Pessoa.

Other news from Brazil was dismal. Brazil's president and his cohorts, Delfim Neto the economics guru among them, tried to distract Brazilians with the "Brazilian Economic Miracle" – the Transamazonic, Itaipu Dam, the Rio-Niterói Bridge – in short, the big "cake" to be baked with slices of prosperity promised to all. They also chased down terrorists and suspects from the Left, interrogating them, imprisoning them, and in a few cases torturing them to death. Chico Buarque was right with his prognostication of hard times to come.

ABOUT THE AUTHOR

Mark Curran is a retired professor from Arizona State University where he worked from 1968 to 2011. He taught Spanish and Portuguese and their respective cultures. His research specialty was Brazil and its "popular poetry in verse" or the "literatura de cordel," and he has published many articles in research reviews and now some sixteen books related to the "Cordel" in Brazil, the United States and Spain. Other books done during retirement are of either an autobiographic nature – "The Farm" or "Coming of Age with the Jesuits" - or reflect classes taught at ASU on Luso-Brazilian Civilization, Latin American Civilization or Spanish Civilization. The latter are in the series "Stories I Told My Students:" books on Brazil, Colombia, Guatemala, Mexico, Portugal and Spain. "Letters from Brazil" is an early experiment combining reporting and fiction, and "A Professor Takes to the Sea I and II" is a chronicle of a retirement adventure with Lindblad Expeditions on the National Geographic Explorer ship. "Letters from Brazil II" is a continued experiment in combining fact and fiction, but now more fiction.

Published Books
A Literatura de Cordel. Brasil. 1973
Jorge Amado e a Literatura de Cordel. Brasil. 1981
A Presença de Rodolfo Coelho Cavalcante na Moderna Literatura de Cordel. Brasil. 1987
La Literatura de Cordel – Antología Bilingüe – Español y Portugués. España. 1990
Cuíca de Santo Amaro Poeta-Repórter da Bahia. Brasil. 1991
História do Brasil em Cordel. Brasil. 1998
Cuíca de Santo Amaro – Controvérsia no Cordel. Brasil. 2000
Brazil's Folk-Popular Poetry – "a Literatura de Cordel" – a Bilingual Anthology in English and Portuguese. USA. 2010
The Farm – Growing Up in Abilene, Kansas, in the 1940s and the 1950s. USA. 2010
Retrato do Brasil em Cordel. Brasil. 2011

Coming of Age with the Jesuits. USA. 2012

Peripécias de um Pesquisador "Gringo" no Brasil nos Anos 1960 ou 'A Cata de Cordel" USA. 2012

Adventures of a 'Gringo' Researcher in Brazil in the 1960s or In Search of Cordel. USA. 2012

A Trip to Colombia – Highlights of Its Spanish Colonial Heritage. USA. 2013

Travel, Research and Teaching in Guatemala and Mexico – In Quest of the Pre-Columbian Heritage

Volume I – Guatemala. 2013

Volume II – Mexico. USA. 2013

A Portrait of Brazil in the Twentieth Century – The Universe of the "Literatura de Cordel." USA. 2013

Fifty Years of Research on Brazil – A Photographic Journey. USA. 2013

Relembrando - A Velha Literatura de Cordel e a Voz dos Poetas. USA. 2014

Aconteceu no Brasil – Crônicas de um Pesquisador Norte Americano no Brasil II, USA. 2015

It Happened in Brazil – Chronicles of a North American Researcher in Brazil II. USA, 2015

Diário de um Pesquisador Norte-Americano no Brasil III. USA, 2016

Diary of a North American Researcher in Brazil III. USA, 2016

Letters from Brazil. A Cultural-Historical Narrative Made Fiction. USA 2017.

A Professor Takes to the Sea – Learning the Ropes on the National Geographic Explorer

    Volume I, "Epic South America" 2013 USA, 2018.

    Volume II, PART I - 2014 and PART II – 2016 "Atlantic Odyssey 108"

Letters from Brazil II – Research, Romance, and Dark DaysAhead. USA, 2019

Professor Curran lives in Mesa, Arizona, and spends part of the year in Colorado. He is married to Keah Runshang Curran and they have one daughter Kathleen who lives in Albuquerque, New Mexico with husband Courtney Hinman. Her documentary film "Greening the Revolution" was presented most recently in the Sonoma Film Festival in California, this after other festivals in Milan, Italy and New York City. Katie was named best female director in the Oaxaca Film Festival.

The author's e-mail address is: profmark@asu.edu

His website address is: www.currancordelconnection.com

Printed in the United States
By Bookmasters